Living *with the* Hawk

Praise for Robert Currie's Writing

"... he has a sense of the particular that constantly surprises, and he makes the dilemmas of his adolescents fresh and specific ... Robert Currie has created a portrait of a place and the people living in it that is very real." — *Toronto Globe and Mail*

"Currie, who taught in Moose Jaw for 30 years until he retired, brings to *Mr. Cutler* a feeling of authenticity and a love of teaching that you know is real ... You care about the teachers and the students, even the bad ones. This is the sign of a true storyteller." — *Regina Leader-Post*

"*Teaching Mr. Cutler* is [Currie's} first novel and it's a dandy ... Currie is most impressive in showing what goes on in Brad's English classes. It's one thing for a teacher to make a lesson exciting for a class of students, but it's quite another for a writer to make a lesson exciting for a reader, and Currie succeeds admirably." — *Winnipeg Free Press*

"Just like real classrooms, this tale offers moments of crackling tension as well as flashes of high drama and high humour. Currie's deft touch with dialogue eases the story along as the hapless but dedicated young teacher lurches from crisis to crisis." — *Saskatoon StarPhoenix*

LIVING *with the* HAWK

ROBERT CURRIE

thistledown press

Thistledown Press Ltd.
118 - 20th Street West
Saskatoon, Saskatchewan, S7M 0W6
www.thistledownpress.com

Library and Archives Canada Cataloguing in Publication

Currie, Robert, 1937-

Living with the Hawk / Robert Currie.
Issued also in electronic format.
ISBN 978-1-927068-39-7
I. Title.

PS8555.U7L59 2013   jC813'.54   C2013-900961-2

Cover and book design by Jackie Forrie
Author photo by Larry Hadwen
Printed and bound in Canada

Canada Council for the Arts   Conseil des Arts du Canada   SASKATCHEWAN ARTS BOARD   Canadian Heritage   Patrimoine canadien

Thistledown Press gratefully acknowledges the financial assistance of the Canada Council for the Arts, the Saskatchewan Arts Board, and the Government of Canada through the Canada Book Fund for its publishing program.

LIVING *with the* HAWK

This book is dedicated to Gwen — with love.

PROLOGUE

When I was in grade nine, two friends and I tried out for the football team. Man, if I had known how that would change everything, I would've joined the stupid yearbook club, or volunteered to clean chalk brushes after school, beat the snot out of them day after day. And told everyone I was an only child, an orphan. See how well my brother and my parents managed by themselves.

So many memories from that fall are bad. And not just bad, horrific. I'd forget them if I could, but I'm afraid they're always with me, at night especially when I lie in bed, twisting and turning, the dark ceiling above the bed like a screen where the same scenes play themselves out, again and again, whether my eyes are shut or open.

Memories have a sly way of inserting themselves between the lines of text books, of hiding behind gruelling homework assignments and leaping out when you've dropped your guard. They can come at any time, I know, in any order, and maybe what I really need to do is lay them out in the precise sequence that they happened, lay them out and examine them, try to find a way to deal with them, see if it isn't possible to have whole days go by without those memories stirring.

The nights, of course, may be another thing.

ONE

On the first day at football practice, all the players spread out across the field and slowly walked through the scrubby grass from one end zone to the other, our eyes on the ground before our feet. Every time we spotted a rock, we picked it up and heaved it off the field. After that there were calisthenics and drills, then blocking and tackling. When I was the only grade nine who made the team, I was ecstatic. I liked to think my success was because I was faster than any other kid when we drilled at running backwards, a perfect skill for a defensive back, but there might have been more to it than that.

What I always remember was Todd Branton, one of the hotshot grade twelves, saying, "Rookie, you are such a lucksack. You made the team because your brother's the quarterback. And that's the only reason." His voice low and sarcastic in the murmur of the locker room, exhausted players on the bench beside him raising their heads to stare at me, wondering what I'd do. And oh no, I couldn't keep my mouth shut.

"Sure, Branton, and you made the team because every time the coaches want to take a dump they know you're there to wipe their butt." The other players still stared at me, a few of them grinning, though you could see they didn't want to.

"Up yours, dirtbag," said Branton. "You smile and I'll rub it off with my jockstrap," but he was too tired to act. Or so I thought. There's something about this Branton — I don't know exactly, but if a fart had a face it'd look just like him.

The next day, getting ready for practice, I had stripped down to my jockey shorts when they came for me, a bunch of them grabbing me at once, lifting me off the bench, pinning me into a metal chair, my brother standing by, grinning — nervously, I thought. He didn't make a move to help me. The screech of duct tape unrolling, and they were tying me to the chair, binding my legs to the chair legs, wrapping tape around and around my arms, securing me to the metal frame. Behind me, I heard my brother say, "This must be a new one. Makes one hundred and ninety-two uses for duct tape."

"And here's number one ninety-three," said Jordan Phelps. He always looked stern — preoccupied, maybe, but he was smiling now. "We can tape his pecker down — so it won't rise up and stand at attention when he sees all those hot bodies bouncing around the gym."

Braying laughter until four of them lifted me and carried me down the hall, opened the door to the gym where the girls' volleyball games were being played. They set me inside and left me there.

Some memory that. I used to lie in bed at night, muscles aching, shins and shoulders bruised, remembering how the cheering petered out, fans one by one noticing me, starting to point, snickering at the naked kid covered only by his skimpy gotch. I knew I was blushing, my ears blooming red, the colour spreading like wild rose petals unfurling in a fast-frame nature movie. There was laughter now, guffaws, one fat kid laughing so hard he was hiccupping and gasping for breath. The volleyball players stopped their game to see what was going on, a tall native nudging the girl beside her and pointing at me, the two of them grinning, the referee finally blowing a whistle, trotting into the gym office, returning with a pair of scissors to cut me free.

~·~·~

When I think about everything that happened, it's kind of ironic that my brother and I started playing football to please our father, then discovered we liked the game, the physical contact, the sudden bursts of exertion. Our father is Paul Russell, a father in more than the usual way, for he served as the Anglican priest at St. David's Church in Palliser when I was growing up. Still does, in fact. Palliser, of course, lies along the Trans-Canada highway on the Saskatchewan prairie, a city of thirty thousand, too short of industries and too near Regina to ever hope to grow. My father claimed it was a nice city in which to have a parish, a good place to raise a family. At least he used to make that claim.

My father always wanted his sons to play sports. When I was in elementary school, he put together a softball team from all the boys in the parish. Even then, I knew that he loved taking off his white collar, rolling up his sleeves — his biceps thick and hard — hitting flies for us to shag in the outfield. Once, when my mother had been using the car and came to pick us up from practice, I saw her behind the backstop, watching him toss balls into the air and slam them out to us. I wondered if she was impressed with the way he hit every ball so high and far that we always had to run to make a catch. Later that night, when they were in the living room and I was sitting at the kitchen table, having a bedtime snack of cinnamon toast and milk, I heard her tell him, "You know, Paul, sometimes I swear you're proud of having hairy arms."

He laughed. "Well," he said, "I've never heard you object to being held in these hairy arms." He must have moved toward her then because I heard the springs squeak in the couch.

"No. I'm serious," she said.

"Well, Barbara, I guess you've got a point to make." I knew at once that something was up; he usually called her Barb. "You going to tell me what it is?"

"Oh, I don't know, but when you're out with the boys like that, playing some game, it's . . . well, it's as if you're showing off."

I was surprised when I heard my father's answer. "Maybe, I am," he said. "Maybe that's exactly what I'm doing."

"Paul!"

"Listen, now," he said. It was what he told Blake and me whenever he wanted to make a point. "About once a week you tell me that being a preacher's wife is no easy task. People always watching your every move. Okay — maybe once a month, but you know what I mean. Being the preacher isn't a whole lot better. Oh, I know, most of the women are all right. It's the men — sometimes they're the ones who get to me. A man of the cloth, they seem to figure, he's hardly a man at all."

"Now, Paul — "

"Oh, they don't come right out and say it, but they think it all right, some of them, you can bet on that."

In the kitchen, washing down the last of my toast with milk, I began to think I was listening to something I shouldn't be hearing, but I wanted to know where this was leading.

"Once in a while," said my father, "I have to remind them I'm not just the fellow who offers them the host on Sunday mornings."

"They know that, Paul."

"They do, eh? You weren't there at the start of practice. Roger Phelps comes up to me, wants to know who's going to coach the kids. I tell him I figure I'll give it a try, and you know what he says? You sure you can handle this? As if I haven't played ball all my life."

"Roger Phelps is a jerk," said my mother. "Everybody knows that. The other men wouldn't think like him."

"Oh no? Couple of the fathers came early to pick up their boys. Looked mighty surprised when they saw me hitting flies."

I got up then to get a fresh carton of milk from the fridge, but my mother heard me. "Blake?" she called. "Blair? It's time for bed."

"It's me," I said. "Just having a shot of milk." Blake wasn't even home yet. My mother named both of us, of course. I guess she thought similar names sounded cute or something. Perfect names for preacher's kids maybe. It's lucky we weren't twins. I'd hate to think what she would have called us then. Louie and Dewey, say, or Timmy and Tommy — something sure to get us creamed at school.

I poured myself half a glass of milk and took a swig. The living room was quiet for a moment; then I heard my father's voice, gruff and louder than usual. "I was just grumping, Blair. You forget anything we said about Mr. Phelps."

"Okay." I belted down the rest of the milk and put the carton back in the fridge. After I switched off the kitchen light, I stood there in the dark, the fridge humming beside me, the sound like a truck at night on a distant highway, but they were through talking. I went up the stairs to bed.

~·~·~

That August before I went into grade nine, I was thinking a lot about high school, wondering what it would be like in a three storey building with six hundred students, most of whom I didn't know. Blake was going into grade twelve, being groomed to quarterback the football team, already a B. M. O. C. according to my father — Big Man On Campus was what he meant — although every time he said it, I thought there was a touch of irony in his voice. He wanted his boys involved in manly sports all right, but he didn't want us showing any signs of swelled heads. "Christ," he once said, "could walk on water, but you never heard him boast about it." I don't think he understood Blake at all. If Blake was ever swelled up with himself, it was a case of being puffed up with excitement because, after two years of spot duty, coming in late in games that were already won or lost, he'd be playing first string. He wouldn't be just a preacher's kid — a PK — but a quarterback, somebody who didn't have to prove he was one of the guys. My father should have known that.

Then again, maybe my father did know it. He was probably concerned about keeping Blake on track, worried about the balancing act that he would have to perform, being one of the guys without ever forgetting that he was a PK too — and ought to live like one.

A balancing act was what it was, no doubt about it. I remember Blake telling me about his first high school dance, the freshie dance when he was in grade nine. The grade twelve student who'd complained all week about being his partner for freshie activities had snuck a bottle into the dance, then in the middle of the crowd back in the darkest corner of the gym he'd brought it out, offering Blake a drink of gin. Blake had stood there, shaking his head, uncertain what to say, the older boy thrusting the bottle at him, telling him it was just a girlie drink, even a preacher's kid could handle it. When Blake said he didn't drink, he'd never had a drink in his life, the boy grabbed him by the front of his shirt, pulled him so close, Blake said you could smell his breath, it was sickly sweet, like he'd been drinking some fancy French cologne.

"You're gonna have a shot of this, right now," he told Blake, "or I am going to pound you in the face. That's your only choice, preacher's boy." Then a malicious laugh. "Either that, or you can ask God to rescue you."

That's when someone spoke up from the middle of the crowd around them. "No need for God. He's got friends."

While the older boy was turning to see who had spoken, it was Jordan Phelps who darted in, Jordan who had spoken, Jordan just a freshie himself who now grabbed for the bottle in the boy's hand and at the same time hacked him on the wrist with a rabbit punch that broke his grip. With gin slopping around him, Jordan bent down and sent the bottle spinning across the dance floor, aiming it towards the far wall where one of the teachers on dance duty was standing. The older boy took a couple of steps after the bottle, thought better of it, turned around, scowling, ready to lash out with his fists, but by then the kids were dispersing, melting into the shadows, all of them getting as far from him and the bottle as they could. The preacher's boy had gotten away, and Jordan too.

Football practice started the week before school, but Blake had spent much of August dragging me down Thirteenth Avenue to the green-space where there was room to throw the long bomb. I was expected to run under his passes and get my hands on them even if I seldom caught them. Once, when I was running flat out, stretching so far I was almost tripping, the ball hit me in the hands and I somehow managed to pull it into my chest without falling. I trotted back to Blake and tossed him the ball.

"That was quite a show," he said. "You should come out for the team." He seemed to mean it too.

"Come on. You're the guy who says I've got hands like bricks."

He laughed. "You're good at knocking the ball out of the air, all right. You could maybe play defence." There was no danger of getting a swelled head with Blake around, but he went on. "It helps to be on a team, to know some guys. Keeps people off your case. Besides, you make the team, Dad'll be impressed."

"You never played in grade nine."

"No, but you could. You might enjoy it." He wasn't looking at me but at the ball, which he held balanced in the palm of his hand. He gave it a spin with his fingers, watching it rotate till it began to topple and he grabbed it with both hands. "Go down fifteen yards," he said, "and cut sharp to the right."

The day that Arnie Winkler, Evan Morgan and I — grade nines all — signed out our football equipment for the first serious practice, we were excited and got there early. No, maybe it was more nerves than excitement, but we were the first ones in the equipment room. Shoulder harness, helmets, bucking pads, jerseys, pants, everything was provided by the school — except, of course, for jockstraps and cups, which we had bought ourselves. I remember sitting in the locker room, my jersey pulled over my shoulders, thinking I looked pretty good, too bad that cute girl who sat two seats behind me in English class couldn't see me with shoulders like this. Arnie and Evan were kind of horsing around, taking turns hammering each other on the pads, just to see how good it felt, my brother and some of his friends arriving with their equipment when Jordan Phelps walked in.

He didn't say anything at first. Just looked at Arnie and Evan, until they quit belting one another, their arms suddenly hanging awkward at their sides, both of them uncomfortable, shuffling, starting to blush.

"You guys," he said, "what a pair of pussies. Gonna really knock someone down, aren't you? Long as it's just each other."

I noticed Blake shoving equipment into his locker. He glanced in my direction, then sat down on the bench, his back toward us, and picked up his football pants, held them on his lap. He grabbed a bucking pad, began to work it into the pocket inside the pants where it would protect his quads.

"Rookies," said Jordan Phelps, "are all big men. Till you get them on the field. Then they hug the bench and pray to God Coach doesn't want them in the game. Wouldn't dare make a tackle — it might hurt a bit."

Blake had another bucking pad cradled in his hand, but he was just holding it, his pants draped over his knee.

"The guys who make this team," said Jordan Phelps, "aren't afraid to take a pounding. They know you've got to be tough, got to wear the other team down, give as good as you get." Although Jordan hadn't moved from where he stood in the centre of the room, Arnie and Evan had backed away, stopping only when they felt the bench at the side of the room behind their legs. They sat quickly down. When Evan glanced at me, I slid along the bench until I was next to them. They didn't seem to be breathing. "Rookies and sluts," said Jordan, "they need to get knocked around some before they're worth a shit."

When I looked for Blake, I saw his pants folded on the bench, a bucking pad on top of them, but he was gone. The sweater in his locker hung slack and crooked, the "C" on the sleeve just barely visible.

~~~

Way back when I was in grade four and my brother in grade seven, Rufus Nickerson was the toughest kid I'd ever seen. The biggest bully too. He lived in a ramshackle house down by the river, the house looking as if it had been nailed together with plywood salvaged from the dump. The backyard was always filled with stripped-down cars and trucks, most of them rusted-out hulks with their hoods open. His dad collected garbage for the city, but people said he could do more with a motor than any mechanic in town. Rufus was in grade eight and he ruled Lord Tennyson Elementary School. Later on, when I was in high school, I wondered if carting around a name like Rufus wasn't what made him so tough — and so quick to pick on smaller kids.

My problem was I didn't figure that out in grade four.

A bunch of us little kids had stayed after school to play in the snow. All afternoon, whenever Mrs. Booker was writing on the board, we'd gaze out the classroom windows, our attention held by the thick snow floating down, the houses on the other side of the schoolyard slowly vanishing in a drifting haze of white. As soon as the bell rang, we threw on our coats and boots, and rushed outside, stamping out a huge pie in the fresh snow of the schoolyard; we were running the circle, playing tag when Rufus walked by and body-checked my best friend, Evan Morgan, into the snow. "Rufus Doofus," I said — under my breath.

Or so I thought.

"Shut your face, kid!" Although he sounded angry, he looked like a starving tramp who'd just been offered a free burger. He tackled me then, drove me backwards, flattened me, landing on top of me, all his weight bearing down. What I remember is gasoline fumes. His clothes smelled of gasoline, and I thought that I would choke. I tried to wiggle free, but he was too big for me. He heaved himself up, got his knees planted on my arms, swearing, leaned towards me, and hawked a gob at my face. I wrenched my head sideways, but it caught me on the ear. Then he laughed and began to slap me. I was squirming and howling, my arms pinned and useless, his gob on my ear, fumes around us like a gas station.

If I'd had a match I would've set him on fire.

And I couldn't even hit back. Worse, I was starting to cry. Like a baby — right there in the schoolyard where everybody'd see me. Both cheeks flaming, eyes stinging, I heard a loud whomp, saw through a blur of tears his head snap forward, a spray of snow and straw like a halo above him, his tuque knocked off, a string of snot swinging from his nose.

He rolled off me, and Blake was there, standing over him, a broom in his hands. A broom. It was at least another second before I realized he must've been at the outdoor rink, playing broomball.

"Don't move," said Blake, his voice surprisingly calm. "You ever touch my brother again, the two of us'll kick the shit out of you. Then I'm gonna hold you down and he's gonna ram this whole broom up your ass. Till it comes out your mouth. Get the idea? Now take off."

Rufus was a good two inches taller than Blake, and I knew he was going to pulverize my brother. When Nickerson stood up, he was breathing hard, his mouth hanging open, as if he was in shock or something. "Who gives a shit about either one of you?" he said. Backing off three steps, he turned around and walked away. Slowly. So everyone could see he wasn't scared at all.

After that, Rufus used to give me the hip whenever he passed me in a crowded hall at school, always just enough of a shove to remind me that he could flatten me anytime he chose, but he never pounded me again and he never crossed my brother. Frankly, I think that Nickerson could've beaten up on Blake too, but he'd never done it before, and when Blake clobbered him with that broom, it knocked just enough doubt into that thick head of his that he didn't want to risk taking a chance and finding out he might be wrong. Blake had a way of raising doubts in people's minds, and for a long time I thought he'd stand up to anybody.

In grade nine, though, I had to wonder.

~~~

Although my brother was the quarterback, there wasn't any doubt that Jordan Phelps was the best player on the team. I was standing on the sidelines, watching the offence and defence scrimmage. My equipment still felt awkward, especially the cup at my crotch. Otherwise, it was much like watching football games from the bleachers when my brother was in grade eleven, except now he was out there all the time, handing off the ball, dropping back to pass. All he had to do was get the ball somewhere in the vicinity of Jordan Phelps and it would be caught. Throw a long looper and Jordan would run under it. Drill it over the line and Jordan would snag the ball between defenders. Anything he touched he caught, and he was fast enough that he could touch almost anything that wasn't knocked down.

I watched a defensive tackle break through the line, forcing Blake to scramble out of the pocket. He was in trouble, running for the sidelines, his receivers covered, until Jordan charged back, giving him a perfect target for his throw.

A hand fell on my shoulder. Hard. "Let's see what you can do out there," said Coach Ramsey. He had a smirk on his face. "Give Ackerman a rest." Morris Ackerman was the cornerback trying to cover Jordan Phelps.

"Coach says to take a break," I told Morris when I trotted out to his position.

"Good luck," he said. "You'll need it."

Blake must have noticed the substitution. The first play he ran was right at me, Jordan charging me as if he were a blocker, me back-pedalling as fast as I could, till he made his move, cutting so sharply that his feet almost went out from under him, the ball already in the air as he stumbled, and I was close enough to get a hand on it, knock it away.

He caught up to the ball as it bounced over the grass, gave it a boot toward the line of scrimmage, then turned to me, a frown on his face. "You were lucky," he said. "But watch out, I'll be back."

I went with him again on the next play, my eyes on him and the quarterback too, but it was okay, the pass to the other side of the field, the ball beginning to wobble — and I was flat on my ass on the ground.

"Clumsy there, rookie," said Jordan.

"You tripped me."

Jordan laughed, no humour in the sound. "Stumbled over your own feet."

On the next play, he came right for me, faked to the left, slammed his fist into my stomach, and went by me so fast I didn't even know I was winded. While I was sucking for a breath of air, I saw the pass was a short one to the other slotback. Someone hauled him down before I could get started in his direction.

I did no better on the next play. Jordan charged me once again, cut to the right when he was almost on me, came back fast, his shoulder in my chest, another fist in the stomach, and he was gone, the ball looping over my head and into his hands as I stumbled backwards, off balance, my feet moving, but not as fast as my body. Then I was on the ground, heaving for air. Bugger nailed me right in the breadbasket. Twice in a row.

"Hey," shouted Blake, "that's my brother."

"You think I don't know that?" Jordan trotted back, glaring him. "Pussy needs to lose some flab."

"Screw you," I said, but I could barely whisper.

The next time he ran at me, I saw his fist coming and chopped his arm away, hard — it had to hurt him — and I was staying with him, but he rammed me, his head down, shoulder slamming into my stomach, my head snapping forward, and down I went. Again. Then another easy catch.

This time when he trotted back towards the huddle, he stopped beside me, reached down, grabbed my hand and pulled me up. "You're okay, Blair," he said.

And I said, "Thanks." Just as if he wasn't the guy who'd been laying dirty moves on me. That was the thing about Jordan Phelps. He could find more ways to treat you like scum and somehow in the end you'd be the one apologizing to him.

That wasn't the worst of it either.

Two

We won four games in a row against easy opponents. Before the first game Arnie had quit football and Evan had been cut, though Coach Conley, our head coach, told him to come out again next year, he'd make the team for sure. I hated to see Evan go, but he just said, "I guess it's up to you now, buddy." Yeah, only grade nine on the team, it was going to be tough. In each of those four games I got onto the field for a few plays as the clock was running down, but that was all. I was about as valuable as a water bottle full of pee, but at least I got to play.

Our fifth game was against Douglas High, a top-notch team, and we beat them 28 to 17. I had a good view of the action, standing on the sidelines, but I never made it into the game. My brother played the best I'd ever seen him play, throwing three touchdown passes, but the other offensive captain, Jordan Phelps, was the real star, catching two touchdown passes and running back a punt for another score. Every time he caught the ball, he brought the fans cheering to their feet as he ran and cut, shifting direction at full speed, tacklers sprawling behind him, awkward hands grabbing at a space he'd just vacated. That day he also added something new. Each time he scored, he ran behind the goal posts and did a forward flip, his hands never touching the ground. The fans loved it, but I thought he was being a hot dog. Coach Ramsey — he was the assistant coach and not a teacher — wouldn't say a thing, of course, but I wondered if Coach Conley would tell him to spread some mustard on it. In fact, when he had us huddle up after the game, he did say something.

Everybody was sprawled on the grass near our sideline, most of the players covered with sweat, their uniforms grass-stained and dirty, a few of them with scrapes and gashes, bloody badges they displayed with pride. I felt like a virgin, not a spot on me or my uniform. I dropped down behind Ivan Buchko, the biggest lineman on our team, crouching low, out of sight.

"Listen up," said Coach Conley. Everybody was so excited with the win, he had to say it again. "We beat a good team today. You deserve to celebrate. No doubt about it. Exuberance after victory's the most natural thing in the world, but anything that looks like taunting of the opposition means you've gone too far. Understand that! We won out there today, because we worked hard to win. We had the right game plan, and we stuck to it — made it work. Good for every one of you." He paused, looked as if he was considering something more, then turned to Coach Ramsey. "Anything to add?"

"Damn right. You guys keep playing like this, you're gonna whip every team in the league. This year is something I been waiting for — this year for sure, we're going to Provincials." Coach Ramsey pumped his fist in the air as he said it, and everybody cheered. I might have cheered too if Ramsey wasn't such a dork.

They were still cheering in the locker room, but now the subject had undergone a sudden change.

"Party-Time tonight!" yelled Vaughn Foster. A huge running back, muscles on him like a teen-aged Arnold Schwarzenegger, he'd scored our other touchdown on a screen pass. Some of the kids said he must be on steroids, but I'd never seen any evidence of that — except for all those muscles — and he did work out with weights in every spare moment. "At my house. The whole team."

More cheers.

"What about your parents?" The question came from Ivan Buchko, sitting in just his jockstrap at the end of the bench. His thighs were massive, a roll of belly fat hanging over them as he slouched forward, his elbows on his knees. He looked like a sumo wrestler waiting for a nine course meal.

"They're going to a dance. Won't be home till two or three. Hell, if they do get home before we're done, no problem, you could flatten my ol' man." Vaughn smiled. He had the kind of smile that made all the girls quiver.

"Yeah, and then you can sit on him," said Jordan Phelps. "Flatten him good. All that weight, he won't be able to do a thing."

Cheers and laughter too, Ivan laughing with everybody else, though you could tell from the glum look of his mouth he didn't think anything was funny.

"Eight o'clock at my place," said Vaughn Foster. "1124 Warren Crescent."

"Okay, you guys." Jordan had something more to say. "This is a team event. We win together and we celebrate together. That means everybody shows up." He looked around the room as if he was the principal handing out detentions to a bunch of frosh. Like King Shit is what I thought, but if he's King Shit, then this is Turd Island, and I didn't much like that idea. Besides, Evan wasn't on the team. There'd be no one to go with me.

Later, after most of us were finished in the showers, Neil Tucker, who was a rookie in grade ten, edged toward me. "You gonna go?" he asked.

I noticed Jordan drying off at his locker, the towel on his hair like a hangman's hood, dark eyes staring out from underneath. Watching us.

Neil was waiting for an answer. A party with Jordan wasn't my idea of a good way to spend Saturday night, but I said, "I guess so. Yeah, sure."

I saw Jordan's teeth flash beneath the towel.

That night at supper — after my father told Blake he looked like the real thing at quarterback, after my mother said he mustn't let it go to his head, after my father added that I'd be good when I got to play more too, after my mother finally set the ham on the table — Blake got busy with his knife and fork, removing a piece of fat from the edge of a slice of ham. I guess he wanted to be done and out of there. He never looked at me. Nor did he look up when my father asked, "What's doing tonight, boys?" but under the table I felt the weight of his foot on mine.

"I don't know," I said, "nothing much, I guess." I knew Blake would kill me if I mentioned the football party. There'd been a bad one last year that a lot of parents were still talking about.

Blake looked at my father then. "There's a new show at the Cap. Supposed to be pretty good."

"Oh yeah, what one is that?"

"A heist movie, I don't know the name. Great chase scene, I hear." Blake put some potatoes in his mouth, was concentrating on chewing. Of course, he hadn't said we were going to the show; he didn't believe in directly lying to our father.

When I approached Blake in his room after supper, he was stretched out on his bed, staring at the ceiling, a wistful look on his face, his hands behind his head. Tacked right above him was Miss April from the Sports Illustrated Swimsuit Calendar. If you looked closely, you could see tiny holes left in the ceiling after he'd been asked by our parents to remove the tacks holding up other pictures. Miss April had more bathing suit and less breast than the other models.

I stood beside the bed until he turned his head and looked at me.

"You going to the party?" I asked.

"Uh-huh."

"You think I should go?"

"Yeah."

"There's gonna be liquor, isn't there?"

"Could be." I knew from the tone of his voice he meant, "Yes."

Sure, and I was going to look stupid because they'd all know I'd never had a drink in my life. Everybody knew preacher's kids didn't drink. Hell, PKs didn't do a thing they weren't supposed to do. At least I didn't. "Evan said something about the two of us going to a show. I sort of promised him."

"So? Catch the early show. You can come afterwards."

"Everybody there's gonna be older than me." Older than me, bigger than me, and girls too, sure as shit, some of them drunk too. If the truth were known, it was almost as if I was afraid to go, but I couldn't very well tell my brother that. "What fun's it going to be?"

Blake swung his legs over the side of the bed and sat up. He faked a quick punch at my face, then nudged me in the ribs with his elbow. "Come for a while. If you don't like it, you don't have to stay. Whole team'll be there."

"Yeah, if they all listen to Jordan."

"Lay off Jordan."

"He's fine — I know — as long as everything goes his way."

"Oh, real cute."

"How come you have to do whatever he says?"

"Go to Hell."

I could see I'd pushed it too far. I tried to look contrite. "Yeah, but the thing is, I wouldn't be drinking."

"No kidding? Two weeks in grade nine and you're not a boozer yet?" He laughed, the sound raw and bitter. "You don't have to drink. You don't have to come either — if you're going to be a pussy."

He'd never called me that before, but I knew where it came from.

"Maybe I'll go, maybe I won't."

I walked out of the room, grabbed the door, ready to heave it shut behind me, but at the last second I held on and let it close with a gentle click.

~·~·~

When the show was over, Evan seemed happy to be heading home, told me no way was he going to come along to any football party, not when they'd cut him from the team, I'd have to go alone.

It was well after nine when I got to Warren Crescent. There were no sidewalks on the crescent, and the street was jammed with cars. I walked on the pavement, trying to pick out the house numbers, but none of them were lit up. It didn't matter though. As I walked farther, I could hear a throbbing bass from a large two-storey house where the crescent turned, the bass booming like the music in those cars you hear coming at you in the night long before you see them. The smart thing, maybe, would be to get out of here and go home.

They'd have the party in the basement, I figured, in the family room — a house this size was bound to have one — so I went around to the back door. The yard was dark, but in the light of a window across the alley I could see two guys sitting on the back fence. I waved at them, but they didn't seem to notice me. They each had a bottle of beer. I wasn't sure if I should talk to them or go inside — or maybe just take off.

I crossed a wooden deck to knock on the door, gave it a good pounding, but no one answered. No wonder, I thought, they wouldn't even hear me with that music hammering away inside. What the heck, might as well go right in.

I turned the knob, was starting to pull at the door, when it swung open, a girl falling into me, her red sweater like a flare in the sudden light from the landing, the music driving in my ears. She grabbed my shoulder, clung there, her breast round and firm against my chest. The smell of beer was everywhere. "Sorry," she said and stepped away, off the back deck, missing a step, staggering as she hit the lawn.

"Doan mind her." It was another girl I didn't recognize. "She's gonna walk it off." The second girl stood a moment watching her friend, then abruptly spun around, almost stumbled back into the house. I hesitated, thinking that was all right, her breast against my chest, before I went gingerly down the stairs behind the second girl. The basement was packed, kids dancing, leaning on the walls, clustered in groups, two couches and three or four chairs clogged with kids. Lots of them I'd never seen before, boys and girls both. The room was dark and full of smoke, the only light coming from behind me on the landing.

"Where you think you're going?" A big guy pushed himself off the wall and came towards me. He wasn't someone from the football team; I was sure I'd never seen him before. "Asked you a question!"

I backed up a step, wondering what to say. The music stopped right then, the CD finished, I guess, and although I mumbled, everybody in the room must have heard me say, "I'm s'posed to be here." Even then I knew it sounded stupid.

"S'posed to be here, eh? Who the hell says so?"

That one I could handle. "Vaughn. He said to come."

"Who the hell's Vaughn?" He stepped into me, grabbed me by the front of my jacket, beery breath on my face.

"Leave him alone." It was Jordan Phelps, his hand on the guy's shoulder, the guy wheeling around, ready to throw a punch, seeing who it was, backing off at once — no hesitation when he saw it was Jordan — the music on again, and he was gone into the crowd. I took a deep breath, the air thick with beer fumes, smoke and something sweet, sickening sweet — Lord, it was probably pot — and I couldn't help thinking, What would have happened if Jordan hadn't stepped in?

"Jeez, I thought he was gonna pound me. Thanks, eh?" I was doing it again, thanking Jordan Phelps. The thing was, I really meant it.

"Don't mind him," he said. "Played last year, and he's missing it. Here, rookie, have yourself a beer."

I shook my head. "I'm not much of a drinker."

"Have a beer." He thrust it at me. I watched the bottle dangling from his hand, red leaf on white label, beer slopping in the bottle, maybe half of it gone — he'd been drinking it himself — the bottle beginning to swing, like a pendulum, against my chest, away, against my chest again.

"Come on, have a belt." The same guy who'd once stood up for Blake with some jerk forcing gin on him, and here he was, pushing beer at me, as if now it was the thing to do.

The bottle swung away, hit me in the chest, hard. I took it from his hand, raised it to my lips, swallowed, the taste so bitter I wanted to spit.

"Have fun, rookie." He was smiling at me now. "I gotta get myself a drink."

Okay, I thought, fine, I'll carry this beer around, but not another sip.

I watched Jordan walk over to a cabinet against the far wall, where a boom box was blasting out the tunes, a cluster of kids opening up to make room for him. He squatted down, pulled a beer from a case on the floor.

"Hi, Blair."

I turned around. It was a girl from my geometry class at school, a little on the porky side, maybe, but real cute. Her name was Joan, I was sure of that, though her desk was way across the room from mine.

"What are you doing here?" I asked.

"I live here."

"You're kidding?" Bright response, eh? Sometimes I'm about as sharp as a wad of Kleenex.

"Vaughn's my brother."

"I didn't know." It was so early in the term I'd never heard her last name.

"He's really going to catch it when my dad gets home."

I looked around the room. Even in the darkness, you could see empty beer bottles everywhere you looked, cheesies and chips on the floor, some of them getting ground into an area rug by the couch, dark liquid spilled on the tile in one corner of the room. "Uh-huh, the place is quite a mess."

"He'll be grounded for a month," she said. "You want to dance?"

"I'm not much of a dancer."

"Who's going to notice here? Come on. All you have to do is shake."

She grabbed me by the arm, and pulled me away from the doorway at the bottom of the stairs. I managed to get rid of my bottle of beer, setting it on a divider by the stairs. Nobody would think a thing about it. The floor was so crowded, you kept bumping someone else, but I discovered it wasn't hard to dance, the beat so loud you kind of felt it, like a drum inside your torso, your feet automatically picking up the rhythm. She was dancing with me, just an inch or so away, looking dreamy-eyed, smiling up at me. Still, I felt like a nerd.

Later on, quite a while later, she stopped dancing, said something to me, but we were right beside the boom box, I couldn't hear a thing.

"What?"

"Got to go to the can."

She pushed through the dancers, heading for a door in the corner of the basement. Feeling stupid, out there by myself, couples gyrating all around, I went after her. She turned the knob, but the door wouldn't open. Someone had beat her to it. She stood in front of the door, the music blaring behind us, and pretty soon, she was bouncing from one foot to the other, like a little kid who's really got to go, but all the while her feet kept perfect time to the rhythm of the music. I had to smile at that. She was about as sophisticated as a kindergarten grad, uh-huh, about as sophisticated as I was myself. After another minute, she pounded on the door. It still didn't open. Then the music stopped, the room hushed in the sudden silence between tunes, and behind the bathroom door we heard someone throwing up.

"I'm gonna pee myself," she said. "Going to the upstairs can." She turned and ran up the stairs.

I was left standing by the bathroom, alone again in a room full of drunks, and it was time to go, man, I wished I was somewhere else. At home, at school, anywhere but here.

That was when the bathroom door opened, the smell of vomit so thick I felt my stomach churn, and out came Neil Tucker, the other rookie on the team. He was staggering, his face a chalky white. "Gotta siddown," he said. He bounced off a couple of dancers and collapsed into a chair, a girl I didn't know trying to escape from the chair, but slow to move, pinned under him for a second until she managed to squirm loose.

He'd walked right past me, so drunk he hadn't even seen me.

Time to get out of here, I thought, and started up the stairs. Laughter below me, shrieks, a girl yelling, "Look at all the puke."

I was out the back door like a shot, the noise and stink, all the crazy people left behind, night air wrapping around me, cool and fresh, but there was laughter in the back yard too, half a dozen guys in a line, arms flung around each other's shoulders, all of them swaying slowly, side to side.

When I saw Jordan Phelps at the end of the line, Todd Branton and Vaughn Foster beside him, I should have known enough to keep going. But no, I was curious, wanted to see what was going on.

I stayed on the left side of the yard, crouching in the shadow of an overgrown caragana hedge, walking on the lawn where the grass would muffle any sound my footsteps made. It didn't matter. The guys were laughing so loud they wouldn't have heard me anyway. When I was parallel with them, I could see someone else — the girl in the red sweater, the one who'd fallen against me when I opened the back door, her breast an instant on my chest — she was sprawled on the grass in front of them, passed out, I guess, her sweater bright even in the dark yard. Just then a light came on in the house next door, and now I could see the guys looking down at her, still laughing, all of them with their dicks out.

They were pissing on her.

"Shut the hell up!" A man's voice, loud and angry. "Or I'm calling the cops."

Their hands were at their flies then, stuffing their dicks inside their pants, but they were laughing still, gasping, hysteria throbbing in their voices as they bumped against each other and backed away. They turned around then and ran for the door.

The last one inside was my brother.

~~~

I lay in bed for hours that night before I finally fell asleep, and then it was tossing and turning, strange dreams that left me terrified and sweating, but I must have dropped into a deep sleep at some point because the floorboards in the hall outside my door always creaked, the sound like the squeal of a mouse having its tail stepped on, and some time that night my brother walked down the hall, across those boards, and I never heard a thing. For a while, later on, I guess, I was trapped in a cave, darkness everywhere and bats wheeling around, you could hear their wings beating the black air, but it wasn't a cave, it was a mine, and the shaft was shrinking, boulders tumbling down to fill it, the entrance blocked, detonations, rock torn from rock, everything collapsing, water pouring in, and my legs wouldn't move, they were pinned beneath me, more explosions, barOOP, barOOP, and I couldn't run away.

I tried to roll over, but my legs were caught in something, the sheet, the sheet twisted and damp, my pyjama collar soaked — I was in my own bed, but the explosions kept coming at me, barOOP, barOOP, the whole house shaking. The room was dark, but when I turned my head I could see numbers glowing inches from my face, the time on my clock radio: 4:03. BarOOP! A pause. BarOOOP! Louder yet, the sound from the wall behind the headboard of my bed. The bathroom wall.

And then I knew it was my brother vomiting. Well, let him suffer. He had it coming, pissing on that girl with all those other jerks. I could picture him on the bathroom floor, hanging on to the toilet bowl as if nothing else connected him with life, gasping for air, the stench of vomit all around him, heaving up the pain from deep within, dry heaves, and nothing coming, nothing but another string of phlegm. Then I heard my father's voice, a mumble through the wall, but Blake just kept spewing.

I knew what it must be like. A few hours before I'd watched the girl in the red sweater throwing up in Fosters' back yard, my hand on her back, patting her, trying to comfort her. My hand wet with urine.

After everyone had disappeared into the house, I'd squatted down beside her, seen that the grass around her face was already stained with vomit. She must've been throwing up before she passed out. I reached for her, touched her shoulder.

"Are you — okay?" Stupid question. She was anything but okay.

No answer. I gave her shoulder a little squeeze, felt her begin to stir. Then she hunched up beneath my hand, a long moan, and she was throwing up again, her body wrung with what I could only call convulsions. I had to do something here.

"What the hell is this?"

When I looked up, I recognized the dark hulk of Ivan Buchko on the back porch. He jumped down and strode toward us, his step quick and purposeful, and I thought, he isn't drunk, maybe he can help me.

"She's awful sick," I said. "We need to get her home."

"Man, she pissed herself."

I hesitated. "Yeah, I guess so." I couldn't tell him — heck, I could hardly believe it myself. "You got a car?"

"Yeah." He shook his head. "I'm not taking her like that."

She had quit throwing up now, but she started to cry, sobs and hiccups mixed together, her body shaking on the grass.

"We can't just leave her here."

Ivan crouched beside us. She was still crying, but she had her hands up by her shoulders now, trying to lift her head from the vomit. "I don't know," he said. "Maybe we could wrap her up in something."

"I got an idea. Stay with her. I'll be right back." I ran for the house.

It took a while pushing through the drunks to find Joan, but she showed me where to look, the second shelf on the landing, and then I was running back across the lawn, my fingers digging at the bag, getting it open, the orange garbage bag flaring out, filling with air as I ran. "We can get her into this," I said. "She won't mess up your car then."

"Okay, yeah."

I knelt at her feet, started to work the bag up her legs, over her wet jeans.

"Wait." He reached down, got his arms under hers, heaved her to her feet, lifted her into the air. "Shit," he said, "she's wet all over. Soaked." But it was easy now. I pulled the bag up and around her, right up to her arm pits.

"I can help you carry her."

"No. Just steady her." He lowered her till the bag hit the ground, me grabbing her shoulders, holding her upright; then with one arm still beneath her armpit, he got the other arm behind her knees and lifted her, stepped away.

"You sure you can manage?"

"Hell yes. Get the gate, will you?"

I started toward the side of the house.

"The back gate, car's in the alley." He began walking, his legs wide apart, her head flopping over his arm. When we got to the car —it was an old Ford, his own car, I guess — he laid her against the trunk, held her there with one hand while he dug in his pocket with the other, fished out the keys. He handed them to me and I opened the back door. Then he lifted her again, turned her around and set her feet on the ground beside the door. As soon as he had her bum on the seat, he dropped her, and she fell backwards, her head bouncing once, something like a snort or a belch erupting from her open mouth as she landed. I lifted her feet into the car and swung the door shut. Handed Ivan the keys. He strode around to the driver's side, opened the front door, turned back to me.

"You get in there with her," he said. "We ain't going nowhere till you shove her head out the window."

I ran around the car, slid in beside her, forced my hands under her, lifting, and pushed her against the window. Held her there and reached across her to get the window open, but Ivan had hit a button, the window purring down. I turned her shoulders, leaned against her, got her head out the window. Ivan drove slowly down the alley. "Where we going?" he said.

"Jeez, I don't know." I didn't even know her name.

"For Christ's sakes, ask her where she lives."

I gave her a shake. "Where do you live?"

A snort that turned into a moan. She was too far gone to answer.

"Come on. What's your address.?"

No response.

"Shit! What am I s'posed to do?" He glared at me in the rearview mirror.

"Maybe if we keep going, cold air on her face, that might do it."

"Fat chance."

I got my arm around her, my hand under her chin, turned her face into the wind as the car bounced out of the alley, picking up speed on the pavement. I felt her chin move in my hand.

"Chew doin'?"

"Where do you live?"

"Leggo me."

"What's your address?"

She mumbled something I couldn't hear, but at least she was talking.

"What?" I slid against her, trying to get my ear closer to her mouth.

I could make out most of it, the words slurred, running together.

"I think she said Avon Drive. Something like that. Twenty-two, for sure."

"Must mean Avord Drive. We'll try that." I was pitched back against her as he swung the car around, making a U-turn in the middle of the block.

"Ohhh! Off-a-me."

"You keep her head out that bloody window."

I was as gentle as I could be, but I held her head out the window till we turned onto Avord Drive, pulling up at a bungalow, the only house in the block with its front light still on. Sure enough, it was number twenty-two.

"Okay. Get her the hell out."

She had her elbows on the doorframe now, her chin cupped in her hands. I went around to her side of the car, lifted her chin and pulled the door open.

"You think you can walk?"

"Feeter tiedup."

"No, you're in a garbage bag."

"Wha . . . ?"

I reached for her feet and lifted them out of the car, pulled her upright. She flopped back against the doorframe.

"Ivan, I think I need a hand."

"No way!" He cranked his head around toward me, but he didn't open the door. "This was your idea, you get her up to the house."

I grabbed the top of the garbage bag, pulled it down, the acid smell of urine stronger now than that of vomit. When she started to lean, sliding sideways toward the trunk, I ducked under her arm, pulled it over my shoulders, wrapped my other arm around her back, and stepped away from the car. She had no choice but to come with me. Her right foot caught in the garbage bag, and I had to force the bag down with my foot, at the same time jerking her away from it. I got her started up the sidewalk then — she wasn't as heavy as I thought she'd be, must've been carrying most of her own weight — and once we were moving, instinct took over, she began picking up her feet, shoving them ahead. Still, the porch light was a long way off.

It was crazy, but with her dragging along against me, I noticed the peonies beside the front porch, and I thought, if they were still in bloom, maybe that would be enough to mask the smell, but they were shrivelled, wasted, their blossoms blown away weeks ago. They looked like old men with shrunken heads, mummified sentinels from an ancient army, left on guard beside a door where there was nothing left to defend. I felt her arm begin to slip from my shoulder.

The door swung violently open, the peonies caught in the sudden breeze, leaning away from the door, as if something awful was coming, something they didn't want to see.

A big man filled the doorway, hair tousled, rumpled grey pyjama top, blue jeans, his mouth twisted in a frown. I stopped when I saw him, almost dropped the girl. He charged toward us, staring at his daughter, a low moan in the air, hers, I thought, but then I saw the way his mouth had fallen open and knew the moan was his.

He reached for her — no, a fist, I tried to back away, but I couldn't let her fall, it caught me high on the cheek, hard as a rock on the side of my face, sparks in my vision, but I managed to turn, swung her between us.

"Bastard!" The word like a cry wrenched from a pet struck by its master.

"Hey!" I heard a car door slam, saw Ivan, a dark hulk at the curb, wavering, my eye filled with tears. "For Christ's sakes, he's trying to help."

A sudden hand on my arm, a claw, yanking me away from her. He held her with the other hand, steadied her against his hip, kicked out at me, but I jumped back, the blow just grazing my shin. When I looked down, I saw that he was wearing brown slippers, his pyjama cuffs sticking out from underneath his jeans.

"Get the hell out of here." His voice fierce, but human now. "I ever see you again, I'll kill you."

I backed away, turned and ran for the car.

Ivan jumped inside, leaned across the front seat and shoved the door open. "Shit," he said, "I think you better get yourself a new girlfriend."

"She's not my girlfriend." My eye stinging. I couldn't tell if he was joking. "I never saw her before."

He roared away from the curb, tires screaming. "Shit, man, I thought he was going to kill you."

"Me too." I put my hand on the side of my face, the whole side throbbing.

"Better take you home."

I started to give him the address, then realized he'd often dropped my brother off, he knew exactly where to go. I sat there, my fingers just touching my cheek, wondering what it looked like. My eye hurt.

Ivan drove through silent streets, both hands on the wheel, no longer speeding, nothing more to say. When he pulled up in front of my house, he turned toward me, patted me once on the shoulder, but he did have another comment.

"That girl," he said, "I don't think she peed herself."

I was already out the door, starting toward the dark house — thank God, my parents were in bed — but I had to stop and speak to him. "Jeez, I don't know, don't know what was going on there."

THREE

Sunday morning at the Russell house was not a time to sleep in. My mother liked to cook a big breakfast, pancakes and bacon usually, while my father went over his sermon one last time in the den. Of course, my brother and I were expected to be up and ready to leave for church when our parents left. That morning, I wondered if my brother would make it. They'd certainly know what happened — my father had heard him, in the bathroom, honking his guts out half the night. Sure, he might've gone in there thinking Blake was sick, but right away he had to know what was really wrong. Maybe, in all that uproar, they'd forget that I had missed my curfew too. I might just get lucky.

As soon as I got into the bathroom, I checked the mirror. Swelling above my cheekbone, the flesh around my left eye a collage of black and blue, a tinge of yellow running through the black, as if some crazy abstract artist had worked it over with a paintbrush. I laid my fingers against the skin. It was tender all right, but it didn't hurt unless I touched it. What was I going to do?

I stayed in the shower a long time, just standing there, the water washing over me, the heat working through me. Maybe it would help my eye, take the swelling down a bit, make the colour fade. Sure, and I used to believe in the tooth fairy too.

When I stepped out of the shower, the bathroom was filled with steam. I could hardly see the towel hanging on the rack. Even after I'd dried myself off, the mirror was fogged up. I wiped it down with the towel, but my face looked exactly the same.

I swung the mirror open, studied the shelves behind it. Toothpaste, shaving cream, after shave lotion, a bottle of perfume, four kinds of deodorant, rubbing alcohol, talcum powder — that might work. I hauled it out, twisted the cap, shook powder into the palm of my hand, ran my fingers through it, began to daub it on the skin around my eye. I turned my head, and leaned toward the mirror. The colours were still there, a lot paler now, kind of sickly looking, but at least they no longer shone.

It might work; it was worth a try.

I got dressed, slacks and a good shirt — I wasn't required to wear a tie — and went down to breakfast.

I sidled into the kitchen, my left side away from my mother who said, "Morning, Blair," and bent to the oven where the pancakes would be warming. My father must still be in the den. I sat in Blake's chair, where the left side of my face would be hidden from my mother. Maybe, if I ate fast enough, I'd be finished before my father came down to eat. When my mother brought the pancakes, I tilted my head away from her while she slid them onto my plate. I could feel her looking at me.

"Stiff neck this morning?"

"What? Oh, yeah, must've slept crooked." I slapped on the butter, poured the syrup.

"You were late getting in."

"I guess I was." Apologize — that was the best approach. "I'm sorry."

"You know about Blake?" she asked.

Before I could answer, I heard footsteps, my father coming down the stairs, and I got my left hand up against my face, started to shovel in the food.

"What happened to you?"

I knew he didn't mean my mother. I looked up at him. He had stopped halfway to the table, a puzzled expression on his face. I was so stupid, so worried about covering up my shiner, I hadn't given a thought to what I ought to say. Didn't have a thing ready. And a fossil, frozen in a rock, could do a better job of improvising.

"I . . . I got hit."

"Who hit you?"

"Some guy — I don't know his name."

My mother almost ran around behind me, bending down to peer at my face. She reached to stroke it, but then her fingers wavered. "Oh, Blair," she said, "does it hurt?"

I shook my head.

"You were in a fight." My father too was shaking his head, as if this was somehow beyond his comprehension. I looked down at my breakfast, pancakes soaked and cooling in a slough of syrup, a gob of butter congealing at the edge of a limp pancake. What could I tell him — that Blake had pissed on a girl and I'd been hammered by her ol' man?

"Well, was it a fight or not?"

I looked up at my father and nodded. My mother gasped and took a step away from me.

His eyes full of pain, my father dropped into his chair. "I don't understand," he said. He ran his hand through his hair, as he always did when something bothered him — an old habit,

I guess, there wasn't much hair left. He glanced at my mother, then back at me. "It's bad enough Blake comes home drunk, but you — you get into a fight. I don't understand this. Life seems normal, we go to bed the same as usual, and when we wake up, everything's changed." He took a deep breath, seemed to steady himself. "What were you fighting about?"

I looked down at my fork, raking it through the butter, trying to mash it into the pancakes, make the butter disappear. "I don't know."

"What do you mean — you don't know?" He was struggling to keep his voice down. "You were there. Of course, you know."

A smear of cold butter, like grease on the soggy pancake. What was the use? I looked up at my father. "It just kind of happened."

"What happened? That's what I'm asking you."

I had to tell him something. Some version of the truth, maybe that would work.

"There was this girl," I said. "She was drunk, throwing up, and I was going to help her, I kind of grabbed her to keep her from falling down, and some guy smashes me in the cheek with his fist." My father was looking at me, his face hard as stone. "It must've been her boyfriend. He was winding up to really let me have it; so I punched him back, nailed him quick before he could hit me again." I don't know where that came from; it was stupid. Maybe, I just wanted to knock that granite look off my father's face, but I made him wince, and then I felt even worse.

"You said you were going to the show." My mother, right beside him now, her voice wavering as if she were struggling not to cry.

"I did. I went to the show. With Evan."

"This didn't happen at the show," my father said. "Were you drinking?"

"I don't drink."

"Listen now," he said. "I want to know exactly where you were."

"I . . . I went to a party. After the show."

"Was Blake there?" my mother asked. "Is that where he got drunk?"

I hesitated. "He was there, yeah. I didn't see him drinking."

"There were kids drinking though, weren't there?" My father rose from his chair, took a step toward me. "Tell me where you were."

I thought of Vaughn Foster and the way he must've caught it from his parents. Oh man, yes. But then I thought of Joan, his sister — she didn't need someone else's father phoning them, getting them all stirred up again.

"Come on, Blair. Whose house was it?"

"I don't know." An outright lie. Sooner or later, I'd pay for that.

"You know where you were. Tell me."

"I . . . I — really couldn't say."

"Paul!" My mother reached toward him, but he wasn't going to hit me, I knew that. He was just angry — angry and frustrated.

"Go to your room," he said. "And stay there. Your brother's grounded, and so are you. Until further notice." He reached for the coffee perk, then shoved it aside. "You bloody well need to tell me where you were." His face was red with anger, but he looked embarrassed too. Bloody, I thought, that was as close as he ever got to swearing. When he spoke again, he sounded tired. "You think about it long enough, maybe you'll come to your senses. I sure hope so."

Some people might imagine I'd be glad of the chance to skip a Sunday service, but the truth is I didn't mind church at all. It was also true that I seldom paid much attention to my father's sermons, my mind drifting aimlessly, but I liked the way his rich voice rolled over me like a bright, warm river, light pouring through the stained glass windows, Christ lambent with colour, the vivid children gathered in His radiance. I liked exchanging the peace, especially with Mr. Hammond — he was a policeman, lean as a fencepost, a tough cop, some people said, but you'd never guess it in church. He was the one who always led the congregation in singing "Happy Birthday," who never failed to look for me, striding down the aisle till he found me, taking my hand in that great mitt of his, holding it, that deep voice saying, "The Peace of Christ be with you, Blair." Saying it and meaning it. And I liked the way we all sang "The Lord's Prayer," some of us kneeling, some of us standing, but all of our voices rising together, merging with the booming peal of the organ, the whole church filling with sound, "For the kingdom, the power and the glory are yours, now and for ever. Amen." And best of all, that moment before dismissal when my father looked down from the sanctuary, spreading his arms wide, until they included us, everyone, and that familiar voice, which was only partly his by then, extended to each of us "The peace of God, which passes all understanding."

Today there'd be no peace for me.

Nor for Blake.

As soon as my parents left for church, I went into his room. His window was thrown up, curtains jumping in the breeze, but still the air held a faint smell of vomit. My brother's eyes were open when I entered, but he closed them right away, his breathing slow and steady.

I was furious with him for what he'd done, enraged with myself for lying to our father. Yes, and blaming Blake for the lie.

"We all heard you last night, you know, honking your guts into the can."

No change in his breathing.

"Come on. I know you're awake." I wanted him to squirm, wanted to see him suffer. "Nice going there, bro. You made Mom and Dad real proud." He rolled away from me, but I wasn't finished. "One good thing about it though, you supplied Dad with enough raw material for a month of sermons. He can talk about the sins of the son for — "

"Go to Hell!"

I looked down at him lying there on the bed, turned away from me, legs curled into a fetal hunch, covers pulled almost over his head, face shoved toward the wall, the bed quivering beneath him. What a sorry specimen, wrapped in blankets and shivering. I wanted to rip the blankets from the bed, make him lie there, shaking on a bare mattress, let him suffer the way he ought to. But I left the room without another word.

He had no idea I'd been in Foster's yard that night, no idea I'd seen exactly what he'd done.

~·~·~

I might have been grounded, but that didn't get me out of helping my mother with the dishes after lunch. She said the dishwasher was full, she'd wash these and I could darn well dry, it would do me good to help out around the house. While she filled the sink with water, I could feel her stealing glances at the bruise on my cheek. I kept my eyes out the window, the backyard lawn covered with a crust of snow, the sky overcast, as gloomy as I felt.

"There goes the squirrel," said my mother, raising a soapy hand to point. Heading for the neighbour's yard, the red squirrel ran along the telephone wire, a circus acrobat, his bushy flag streaming behind him. He disappeared beyond the pine tree in the next yard.

"I didn't see him at the feeder," she added. I kept my mouth shut. Bloody squirrel was as big a show-off as Jordan Phelps. We'd often find him dangling upside down from the lowest branch of the maple, the bird feeder hanging crooked from his weight, his front paws dipping into the tray, retrieving a single oiled sunflower seed, raising it to his mouth.

"Must've been there," she said, nodding at the feeder, ignoring my silence. No birds in the tray. It hung motionless, its green plastic roof speckled white with bird shit, its transparent walls revealing that it was still more than half full of seeds. Beneath the feeder the snow was dark with broken shells. I suppose she'd want me to get out there and shovel them into a garbage bag before a wind scattered them across the yard.

"All the birds are gone," she said.

I studied the maple, its branches bare except for a host of pale yellow seeds that hung like miniature propellers on the ends of southern branches.

Usually when the squirrel was feeding, we'd see the birds perched on higher branches, heads cocked, waiting until the feeder was free, sparrows mostly, but a lot of finches too. Sometimes a pair of chickadees would dart from branch to branch, one of them dropping to the feeder tray, snagging a seed and darting off again, the other following right away, first to the feeder, then flitting out of sight. Often on the ground there'd be juncos, their backs dark as slate, pecking through the mess of shells for seeds spilled by frenzied sparrows. Once a larger bird landed on the tray, its size at least three times that of a sparrow, the feeder tipping beneath it. It was so big it had to sit sideways on the tray. A flicker, my mother said, you could tell by its black crescent bib, the crimson patch on the nape of its neck.

"The squirrel must've made a run at some of them," she said, "chased them all away."

But, no, here was a single bird, hopping from branch to branch, heading for the feeder, no sign of colour on its breast or throat, nothing but a sparrow. It landed on the feeder tray, ducked its head, began to eat.

"Lucky bird," I said. I thought I better say something. "He's got the feeder all to himself."

I heard her gasp before I saw what was coming, the sparrow darting off the feeder, flying straight at our window, a hawk right behind it. Just before the sparrow struck the glass, it veered to the right, and I swear its face was so close to mine I could see panic written there. The hawk veered too, and they both were out of sight. A second later they were back, the sparrow fleeing, swerving, wings frantic, the hawk swooping after it, plucking it from the air, flying up into the maple.

Beside me, I heard my mother moan. Her hand was at her mouth, suds dripping from her chin.

I heaved the window open, leaned toward the screen. "Hey," I shouted. "Get out of here." Immediately felt foolish, the damage already done, the hawk impervious to commands from anyone below. Before I could slide the window shut, I thought I heard a bone snap above us in the maple.

~~~

Part way through Monday's practice, Coach Conley sent me in to play defensive back. I guess I was angry because everything was going as it always did in practice — Blake working behind the centre, in total control as usual, running the same plays as smoothly as ever — just as if Saturday night had never happened, as if things were still the same.

I was supposed to cover the slotback on the short side of the field, but I had something else in mind.

Even before the ball was snapped, I went for him. Nobody between us, and I was going full speed, Blake trying to wheel away, the ball already out of his hand, but I had him, my shoulder in his chest, smashing him backwards, pounding him into the ground, all my weight on him. I felt him bounce beneath me, a great whoosh of air expelled from his lungs.

When I stood up, Coach Ramsey was beside me. "Way to go," he said, but his voice wasn't right. "You're offside, the guy you should have covered scores the touchdown, you wrack up our only decent quarterback, you're a bloody jerkoff."

Coach Conley was kneeling by my brother, Blake still on the ground, gasping, carrying on like a jackfish hauled out of Buffalo Lake. A little wind knocked out of him, that was all. I turned away. A hand grabbed my shoulder, wrenched me around, a finger jabbing my chest. Coach Ramsey.

"I'm talking to you. Don't you ever turn away when I'm talking to you."

"Send him over here, Drew." Coach Conley was still crouched beside my brother, but he was watching us. Blake was sitting up now, breathing deeply, glaring at me. I walked towards them.

"You try that again," said Blake, "I'll break your effing arm."

"You and what army?" I know it was a dumb thing to say. My brother could cream me any time he felt like it.

Coach took my brother's arm and helped him to his feet. "You going to be okay, Blake?"

"Sure. This little pussy couldn't hurt me if he tried."

There was laughter behind me, Jordan Phelps and Todd Branton grinning like fools, Coach Ramsey scowling still.

"*Pussy ,*" said Coach Conley, "is a not a term I'm fond of. Smacks of misogyny." And immediately I thought, man, this is no ordinary coach, he never forgets he's a teacher. He glared at Blake. "You want to play on our team, you won't use it again."

Blake opened his mouth as if to say something, to argue, maybe, but he closed his mouth and kept silent. Jordan and Todd were no longer smiling. Apes. Probably didn't know what misogyny was, but they knew when Coach was angry. He wasn't finished either.

"I don't know what's going on with you two, but you better settle it somewhere else. Doesn't belong on the football field." He stepped away from my brother, put his arm around my shoulder and steered me toward the sideline. "From where I was standing, Blair, that looked a lot like dirty football. Matter of fact, looked like you wanted to hurt your brother."

I hadn't thought of it in quite that way, but when he said it I had to admit that he was right. Smashing Blake to the ground felt plain good. "He had it coming."

Coach lifted the peak of his baseball cap, wiped the back of his hand slowly across his forehead, a damp smudge spreading above his left eye. When he lowered his arm, he seemed for a moment to be studying the sweat on his hand, waiting for it to dry. "Nobody deserves a dirty hit," he said at last. "You ought to know that by now. Thought you did. Well, it'll give you something to think about while you're running. Four laps! Right now. Maybe you'll smarten up by the time you're done."

I headed for the track that ran around the field, but I was thinking of something I'd once heard my father tell my mother, "Even the disciples were far from perfect. Take St. Peter; when it comes right down to it, he was a bit of a misogynist." When they were finished in the den, I'd looked up the word in the big dictionary that always lay open on a stand beside my father's desk.

Was Blake a woman-hater, I wondered, was that what Saturday night was all about? He was far from perfect, oh man, yes, and I had some evidence that Coach would never know.

Still, *pussy* was Jordan's term, his way of nailing anyone who wasn't doing exactly what he thought they should. He used the term a lot, but never when Coach Conley was anywhere around. He was way too smart for that.

≈≈≈

Later in the week, I passed the girl from Saturday night hurrying down the hall at school. No red sweater on her like a flare this time, but a grey shirt, pale and subdued, her head down, the expression on her face subdued too. I don't think she noticed me. Probably wouldn't recognize me anyway. I watched her all the way down the hall until she disappeared into her home room. Another grade nine room. She was no older than I was.

An elbow in my ribs. "Got your eye on someone hot, eh?" Evan Morgan was right beside me, leering.

"Not exactly. But I'd kind of like to know who that is?"

"Yeah, I'll bet you would. Boobs on her like a porn star."

I wondered what Evan was going on about. She was pretty all right, but her boobs were nothing special. I decided to keep it light. "More like a Disney star, I'd say. You don't know her name, eh?"

"Sure. Amber Saunders." He leaned against me, grinning, gave me another jab in the ribs. "I hear she goes for football players."

It was a week before I saw her again. Noon hour on a nice day, warm September sun beaming down, most of the kids outside on the lawn, sucking back on Slurpies and Big Gulps, when I headed for my locker to get some homework I should've finished the night before. I came booting down the stairs, opened the basement door, and stopped.

At the bank of grade nine lockers part way down the hall, I saw Jordan Phelps leaning against a locker, a girl pinned between his arms. He must have just come in from outside, because he still wore his football jacket, the lightning crest on its leather sleeve just visible in the shadows of the hallway. When the girl tried to squirm free, ducking her head beneath his arm, I saw it was Amber Saunders. He was too quick for her, grabbing her shoulder, pushing her back against the locker. He lowered his head then, and whispered in her ear. A stage whisper — I could just make out what he was saying. "Come on, babe, you know you liked it lying there on the grass. Looking up — and all that fresh meat just for you." He laughed, shoving himself against her, rubbing his crotch on her stomach.

The bastard, I thought, and took a step towards them, but just then, from behind the row of lockers, another girl appeared, a native, the one I'd seen playing volleyball. She paused, watching them for an instant, her body rigid, skin tight over high cheek bones, front teeth digging at her lower lip. She took a deep breath and strode toward them.

"Asshole," she said.

I don't think Jordan knew she was there until he heard her speak. As he turned to see who it was, she hit him in the shoulder with her fist, hard, spinning him around — he must've been too surprised to react because before he made another move she was between him and Amber, her knee flying up, catching him right in the groin, and he was falling backwards, the metal locker clanking behind him. She grabbed Amber by the arm, yanking her away from him, the two of them starting toward the stairs, breaking into a run.

"Damned wagon-burner!" Jordan slumped against a locker, both hands pressed to his groin.

They ran past me and up the stairs. Man, I thought, she is something else, tying into him like that — and she's beautiful.

Jordan must have seen me then. He dropped his hands, straightening his back, sliding up the locker till he was upright. His face was dark with shame or anger — yeah, anger would be right. "Bitch," he said, "she's just asking for a good banging." His right hand dangled at his side, knuckles rapping the locker.

If I got my books now, I'd have to go right by him.

Okay, I could do that. Besides, he couldn't know how much I'd seen. I started past him.

"You smile just once," he said, "I'll knock your stupid head off."

And she'd kneed him in the balls, a dark fire in her eyes, blazing still when she came by me.

"You know something?" I kept walking towards my locker. "She had it right — you are an asshole."

The second before I slammed into my locker, I felt his hands flat on my back, driving me forward. I managed to turn my head before I hit, taking the blow on my chest, the locker rigid against me, my cry lost in the collision of body and metal. I swung around, and he was coming at me, both fists ready, and

I was going to get it now, but there, behind him, was my math teacher, Mr. Ambrose, turning toward us, Mr. Ambrose on noon duty, yelling, "Hey! What's going on here?" He marched right up to us, his eyes darting from me to Jordan and back again. "No fighting, you understand?"

Jordan grinned at him — he actually grinned. "Sorry, sir" he said. "We weren't mad — just horsing around is all. Guess, maybe, we got carried away."

"Sounded like someone busting lockers." Mr. Ambrose didn't look convinced. "I catch you two fooling around down here again, it's detention next time. Now clear out."

"Sure thing, Mr. Ambrose." Jordan gave him a little nod as he went by him.

"You heard me." Mr. Ambrose was glaring at me.

"I need into my locker. For my homework."

"Uh-huh," he said, "leave it till the last minute, do we?"

He stood there, watching while I opened my locker and dug out my books. I wondered if he'd noticed my fingers shaking as I turned the dial of my combination lock.

FOUR

My brother asked me what the hell I was doing, trying to cream him like that at practice, the snap barely in his hands when I hit him.

"You don't like getting hit," I said, "maybe they'll take you on the chess team."

"Up yours. You were a mile offside. Besides, you hit like a cream puff."

We let it go at that. He didn't ask again why I wanted to hit him, and I wasn't going to tell him. If he had half a brain, he probably knew why. Neither of us spoke of what had happened that Saturday night on Fosters' back lawn. In fact, we seldom talked anymore — except, of course, at meals. We both thought it politic to strive for something like normal conversation in the presence of our parents, but at supper that night, I wanted to talk.

As soon as our father had asked the blessing, I said, "Guess what? There's a native girl at school."

My mother was passing around the bowl of potatoes. She paused, a little gob of potato stuck on her thumb. She set the bowl down in front of me, wiped off the potato with her serviette. "Only one?" she asked. "I understand in Regina some of the inner city schools have more natives than whites."

"She's the only one I've seen. Don't know who she is, but I saw her in the hall again today at noon. She's . . . kind of pretty."

"Anna Big Sky," said my brother.

"You know her?"

"Sure. She's in my history class." He cast a quick glance at my father, and for some reason I thought of a swimmer standing at the edge of a pool, stretching out his toe to test the water. "The guys," he said, "some of them, call her Anna Big Boobs."

"Blake!" It was my mother who spoke first. My father finished chewing something, swallowed, set down his fork. "Listen now," he said, glaring at Blake. "That's no way to talk. Not at this table — and not at school either."

"I don't call her that," said Blake. He looked as if he wished he'd kept his mouth shut. "I'm just saying what the guys say. Some of them."

"Some of them need to smarten up," my father said, "and not be putting women down. Natives either."

"Natives," Blake said, "they don't pay taxes, you know." He looked angry, but surprised too. I wondered if he was trying to get a rise out of our father, if he'd said more than he intended to say.

"Enough!" said my father. "Now pay attention, both of you. Living in Palliser, there isn't a reserve within a hundred kilometres. Result is: people don't have much experience of aboriginals. You don't know — "

"I know Anna," said Blake. "She's sharp as anyone in class. Got guts too."

He was backtracking now, making up for his last comment, sure, but he already knew her, and I didn't. I felt a rush of heat somewhere inside, a flash of jealousy, perhaps, but that was crazy. Why would I be jealous? Besides, she was three years older than me. I wouldn't have a hope with her.

"What I was going to say," — my father fixed Blake with a cold eye — "is this: you don't know what it was like. All those native kids carted off to residential schools — parents crying, kids crying, government saying this is how it's going to be, and we Anglicans, we went along with it, ran some of the schools, tried to make a home for them, but it didn't work. It should've, maybe, but it didn't. Some of those kids would get up at night, look out the dormitory window, see the smoke drifting from the chimneys of their own homes. Sometimes their homes were that close. They knew their parents were sitting around the fire, but they couldn't go there. Huh, might as well have been in prison." My father leaned towards Blake, his supper forgotten. I could tell he was warming to his subject. "On no, the bloody government wouldn't allow anything like that. Got to knock their culture out of them, teach them the white man's way. Those residential schools — "

"We know," said Blake. "Mr. Helsel's got all kinds of clippings from the papers. He has us read them every time you turn around." Blake looked at our father and decided to back off, to keep quiet.

"Whole generations of aboriginals cut off from their parents," said my father. "Never had a chance at family life, no chance to see how it is that parents go about raising kids. No wonder some of them have problems."

"A lot of them have problems," my mother said. She nodded her head towards my father's plate, his cooling food.

"You talking about Fort Qu'Appelle again?" But he scooped up a forkful of potatoes — he was finished speaking at us. Sometimes I wonder if other ministers are like that, so used to sermonizing they sometimes can't resist dropping in a sermon when it isn't Sunday morning.

She nodded her head. "Our house was too close to the Fort Hotel. Growing up, I saw a lot of things I'd just as soon forget about. Saturday nights and the beer parlour. Like I said, a lot of them have problems."

"Yes," said my father, "I suppose you're right. Doesn't say much for the way we handle problems, does it?"

Then I thought of Anna Big Sky; if she had problems, I bet she'd know how to handle them. Maybe the next time I saw her in the halls I'd speak to her. Tell her how brave I thought she was, taking on Jordan Phelps the way she had, how beautiful she was. Yeah, fat chance of that. Get close to her, I'd be sputtering away, someone might just as well bind my tongue into a reef knot.

"That native girl," said my mother, "it mustn't be easy for her at school. By herself, I mean."

"It isn't," said Blake. "Some people give her a rough time because she isn't white — but man, she's got a temper, tells them where to stick it. Doesn't hold back either. Anybody else she treats . . . well, the same way everybody does." There was a warmth in my brother's voice. For some reason, he made me think of Mr. Salter at church, whose wife had died, who liked to visit with my father, who was so lonely he always steered the conversation in the same direction so he could talk about his wife. "I'll tell you something though; nobody gives her a rough time in Mr. Helsel's class. Anybody did, he'd slap them in detention the rest of the year. He figures natives get a raw deal in this country, he sure isn't going to let that happen in his class."

"You mean he favours her?" My mother looked thoughtful.

"Oh no. History class, everybody's got to work their butts off — her included, but you can tell he kind of likes her."

"I don't blame him," I said.

Blake gave me a sarcastic look. "What do you know about it? You've never even met her." He jerked his head toward me so violently that I flinched and immediately felt foolish. "I don't think she's got much background in Canadian history, but she works hard and she catches on real quick. Sits right at the front where she won't miss a thing." He turned to me again. "Right next to me," he said, and I knew he was rubbing it in.

"Oh ho," said our father, "and I thought you liked to hang out with the boys in the back row."

"Not in history class. Fool around there, you end up dead in the water."

"You fool around anywhere," my father said, "your marks are going to suffer." My father glanced at Blake, and then at me, nodding his head. He could never resist the chance to make a point he thought would be good for his sons to hear. Yes, and my marks weren't as high as Blake's. With both of us grounded though, we'd have lots of time for schoolwork.

"The thing about Anna," my brother said, the same warmth in his voice as before, "is she sat at the back the first day she transferred in. Todd Branton leans across the aisle and whispers something to her — I don't know what it was, he can be a real jerk — and you know what? She slaps him on the mouth: At the start of class. Then she marches up to the front and takes a seat there. Now here's the good part. Mr. Helsel was right there at the front of the room, saw the whole thing. You know what he says? 'Todd,' he says, 'I think we'll have a little chat after school.' Cool as anything. You've got to hand it to him."

"And to her," said my mother. "It's nice to know she's not going to put up with things like that."

"She won't take any crap." My brother grinned. "That tends to make most people kind of reluctant about dishing out the crap."

"Guff," said my mother. "*Crap* is not a term we need to hear at the dinner table."

After supper, when our parents had gone to the front room and we were stacking dishes in the washer and cleaning off the counter, I spoke to Blake, keeping my voice low, so it wouldn't carry to the other room. "You've got a crush on her."

He turned toward me, a pot in his hand. I got the feeling he would have liked to bounce it off my skull. "She's aboriginal," he said, but there was a glint in his eye, a darkness. I wasn't sure what he meant. "Besides," he added, "I think maybe you're the one with the crush." He pulled out the washer's bottom tray and moved a bowl so he could fit the pot into the corner. When he spoke again his voice was cold. "Say, smart guy, how'd you like practice today?"

~~~

Coming into the locker room after school that afternoon, I'd taken care to keep my distance from Jordan Phelps. When I arrived, he was sitting on the bench before his locker, pants and shoulder harness on, but he made no move to pull on a jersey. He seemed content to sit and watch Vaughn Foster hunched beside him on the bench, doing bicep curls with a barbell he kept in his locker. Jordan didn't even glance in my direction, but I got the feeling he knew I was there.

Vaughn had a sheen of sweat on his right arm before Jordan spoke. "You ever think about that hot Anna Big Sky?" he asked. "I hear she puts out for guys with lots of muscle."

"Oh yeah, sure thing." Vaughn grinned, with embarrassment, I guess, and somehow it made him look even more like a guy the girls would go for. He switched the weight to his left hand.

"Think about it. Those Indian girls go like minks. By the time they're twelve, they're all putting out."

What a crock, I thought, but I didn't say a word.

The weight kept rising, falling, the pace steady, Vaughn trying to ignore him.

"You know what the experts say. A little red meat is good for the appetite."

I got suited up as fast as I could and headed for the field.

When we'd finished warming up and doing drills, while Coach Conley was working with the kickers at the other end of the field, I noticed Jordan go up to Coach Ramsey. He was talking to Ramsey, but he was grinning at me, and I could hear every word he said.

"Why don't you put young Russell in? He never gets much chance to play in game situations."

They put me on the corner, and, watching the team gather for the huddle, it was the same thing again, Jordan talking to Blake this time, but grinning at me. I wished I could hear what was going on because, pretty soon, Blake was grinning too.

I figured there'd be a pass in my direction, and when Jordan didn't try to fake me I thought he was going deep. He hit me while I was still back-pedaling, his shoulder in my chest, and I stumbled, felt his helmet now, under my chin, driving me backwards, and I was flat on the ground when Blake galloped by, the ball cradled at his side. He'd called a run for my side of the field.

"Hey, Russell," said Coach Ramsey, "you're supposed to nail the runner, not wave bye-bye while he scores an easy touchdown." He called to Blake: "Run that play again."

This time when Jordan came for me, I tried to cut around him, but he veered with me, like a hawk swooping, striking its prey, and I was on the ground again.

They ran it six times in a row, Jordan hitting me every time, hammering me as hard as he could, using the helmet every chance he got, though once I managed to dodge around him, and here was Vaughn Foster blocking too, ramming me aside just as Blake darted by. It was kind of weird, but when Jordan trotted back for the next play, he never looked at me, but I heard him say, "You know something, Russell? You're a tough little sucker." Then he paused beside me. "Your brother's being a jerk. I'll have him call something else."

He wasn't the only one with something to say to Blake. I hadn't noticed it before, but Coach Conley had left the kickers to their work and was standing on the sidelines beside Coach Ramsey, drawing one foot back and forth in the chalk at the fifty-yard line. He didn't seem interested in watching the action. Suddenly, he stepped onto the playing field, cupped his hands around his mouth and called, "You've got that play down just fine, Blake. Time to work on another one." Then he was walking toward me.

"You want to sit out a couple plays?" he asked. I couldn't tell if he admired my effort or felt sorry for me.

"No, no," I said, "I'm fine." But my legs were weak, I was shaking like a kid before his first communion.

~·~·~

It was the very next day that I ran into Anna Big Sky at school. I guess I'd have to admit that "ran into her" isn't the most accurate term for how we met. My brother had said she was in his history class, and I knew he took history in period four. When the bell rang to start the five minute break, I took off, running for the history room, hoping to catch her before she disappeared into the jumble of kids that always jammed the halls between classes. At first I thought I'd missed her — the doorway was empty — but then she came striding from the room, a backpack slung over one shoulder.

"Excuse me," I said. Already I felt like such a kid. "You're Anna Big Sky, aren't you?" That was obvious. I was going to have her convinced I was a complete idiot. Yeah, put me near a girl I liked and you might as well jam my brain through a garburator.

"So?" She stopped beside me. She was an inch or two taller than I thought she'd be, uh-huh, taller than me.

"I just wanted you to know I saw you yesterday — at noon with Jordan Phelps." Her lips were drawn together, a thin, tight line, her expression stern. "He's a great athlete, you know." Why was I telling her that? I rushed on. "But he's a total jerk. He had it coming." Her lips relaxed a bit, but she didn't smile.

"And who are you?"

"Blair Russell." I was surprised how good it felt just to think that now she'd know my name.

"You must be Blake's little brother."

I stretched up as tall as I could, my heels lifting off the floor maybe half an inch. "Yeah, but I don't boast about it."

She glanced around as if checking for someone, then leaned toward me before she spoke. "I remember you. The guy with just his gotch in the gym. Nothing else but duct tape and bare skin — mm, and lots of muscles."

She smiled then, white teeth shining between red lips — for just a second I thought she meant it, but that was crazy, she was teasing me. Still her dark eyes were shining too. I think I was in love with her already, but she was moving down the hall.

"I've got a class," she said, reaching behind her with her right hand, groping for the strap on her pack, her breast thrusting forward as she plunged her arm beneath the strap and pulled the pack around. I couldn't help myself; I thought, man, she does have big breasts.

She was striding away from me, and I had to run to catch her. I hoped I wasn't blushing.

"Something else," I said. "Yesterday at noon, I thought you were terrific."

She stopped so suddenly I almost went past her, but I got myself stopped beside her.

"You're okay, Blair." She gazed right at me, her eyes as warm as they were dark. I was blushing now for sure. "Got to hurry. I'll see you around."

She walked down the hall towards her next class, and I watched her all the way, saw her open the glass door at the end of the hall, her good, strong arm heaving it open, saw her go up the stairs, her feet dancing on every step till even they had disappeared from sight.

My name, I thought, it sounded different when she said it, no, not different, special.

But I was late for class.

My father was reading *The Anglican Journal* when I got home from school that day. He dropped the paper on his lap, smiled at me, asked me how my day had been, but his eyes kept dropping to the open paper, and I knew he was in the middle of an article he wanted to finish. That was all right. I wanted my brother in the room when I talked about my day.

I grabbed the latest *Maclean's* from beside the globe on the coffee table and flopped on the couch, idly turning pages until Blake came downstairs. He went to the front door, collected *The Leader-Post* from the mailbox and came back into the room, slapping my legs with the folded paper.

"Shove over," he said.

I sat up, gave him half the couch, waited till he found the sports section.

"Coach say anything when I was late for practice?"

"Didn't notice."

I could see he was into a piece about the Riders, the columnist, Rob Vanstone, trying to stir up a quarterback controversy.

"Maybe I got lucky, and he didn't notice either."

"Probably not."

This wasn't working out the way I'd planned. "Mrs. Young was on my case, kept me after class."

"Mmm." He didn't care.

I heard a rustle of paper, looked across the room at my father, all his attention directed my way. "Tell me: why would she be 'on your case', as you put it?"

"I was late for class." It was okay now. I knew my father, knew exactly what question was coming next.

"And why were you late for class?"

"I got talking to Anna Big Sky." I had to hand it to my brother. He never moved the paper, never turned his head, but I saw the tension in the line of his jaw. He was listening all right. "Time flies when you're having fun, eh? Talking to her, you know, I didn't notice what time it was. She's really neat." Looking at Blake, you'd swear he was cut from a block of marble. No sign that he was breathing. Let's see what I could do about that. "I think she kind of likes me." Not even a tremor.

"But man, I saw the time and took off running. I almost made it." That was for my father.

"Seems to me," he said, "being late isn't something you should be feeling proud about."

My brother was still hidden behind his paper, but now he turned his head and glowered at me. "You got that right," he said.

I might have thought he was responsible if the crap had started the next day, but it didn't begin till later in the week. By then, I'd managed to see Anna Big Sky three more times in the halls at school. She always kept moving, except on one occasion never stopped to talk, but she always spoke. "Blair," she said, just that, never "Hello," or "Good to see you," but with a smile every time, the kind of smile that would melt the ice off the creek the coldest day in January.

I wanted to see her every chance I could — which is why, when we had a short practice that afternoon, I grabbed a quick shower, pulled on my clothes when I was hardly finished dripping, and rushed into the gym. The volleyball games were still going on, her team defending the far court. I trotted across the gym and climbed onto the bleachers. The girls playing in the back row were so close, you could almost reach out and touch them. Anna, though, was in the front row, blocking shots, slamming the ball down at the floor. Man, she knew how to get elevation, her hands rising way above the net while somehow she hung in the air, smashing the ball past another leaping girl.

She'd just scored a point when I saw the far door open. Vaughn Foster sauntered into the gym, strolled slowly along between the stage and the court, then reached out with those powerful arms, hoisted himself onto the stage right beside the net. Bugger, I thought, what's he doing here?

A minute later, Anna was in the back line, taking over the serve. Most of the girls served underhand, but Anna raised the ball above her head, slammed it across the net. It would have gone out-of-bounds, but one of the Vanier players tried to block it, had it ricochet off her hands. Another point and our girls would win.

When Anna got the ball back, she cradled it for a second in both hands, then turned slowly around. Turned around and winked at me. "I need some luck, Blair," she said and shoved the ball toward me.

For a second I didn't know what to do, but then I reached out and tapped the ball with my fist.

"That'll work," she said. She tossed the ball above her head, but this time she leapt to meet it, catching it at its apex, smashing it so hard that it was already coming down as it crossed the net, an instant later hitting the floor, no one even close to it. Anna turned to me again, grinning, her right hand raised, and I slapped my hand on hers — no hesitation now. Man, it was almost as if I'd won the game for them.

The girls clustered together for a cheer, then trotted off the court, all of them passing right in front of the stage where Vaughn Foster sat, slouched there, his elbows on his knees, looking as cool as Brad Pitt would ever look. When Anna was almost beside him, he casually lifted one hand, that handsome smile of his spreading across his face, and she gave him a high five as she headed for the showers. Shit, I thought, why did he have to show up?

I was in the Seven-Eleven at noon hour when it began. Some kid I'd never seen before walking by me in the line-up, muttering, under his breath it seemed, but just loud enough so I'd be sure to hear him, "Injun lover," like that, the kind of thing you might hear in some old clunker of a cowboy movie on the late show, one you'd be too embarrassed to watch if anybody was in the room with you. It sounded so stupid I almost laughed.

I was in the locker room, pulling my practice jersey over my head when it started there.

"You hear about the football player couldn't get himself a girl?" I knew the voice at once — Jordan Phelps. "Had to settle for red meat, eh? Pretty soon he don't want nothing else."

Better ignore him, I thought. And then I thought about his grammar, which was usually good, but this was weird, now he was dumbing it down, playing the part of the folksy redneck. I tugged at my jersey, got it twisted on my shoulder pads. Jordan was sitting on the bench, leaning against his locker, lounging with his feet crossed before him, Todd Branton crouched beside him like a toad. Branton grinned at me. "What the hell kind of guy," he said, "chases after squaws?"

"Screw you." I gave my jersey a yank, heard it tear. It was still caught on my pads, but I walked by them, jerking at it to get it down. Practice jerseys, they were always ripping.

On the bench beside the door I noticed Morris Ackerman and Neil Tucker getting into their equipment. Morris was bent over his shoes, looking glum, concentrating on his shoelaces as if he thought they might somehow tie themselves in knots if his attention lapsed for even a second. Neil just looked disgusted, but neither of them spoke.

On the way out I almost bumped my brother coming in. He was flushed and in a hurry. I kept going.

Things were okay at practice, no one hassling me; I even laid a hit on Todd Branton, nailing him just as the ball touched his fingers, the ball bouncing in the air, him knocked to the ground. It felt good to hit someone. I thought Branton might try another smart crack, but Coach Conley was there. When Branton got up, he jogged back to the huddle without a word, never even looked at me.

I guess he was saving it for the shower room.

Half a dozen guys around me, I was massaging shampoo into my hair when he started. "Stinks in here," Branton said. "Like somebody's been rubbing up against a piece of smoked meat."

I groped for a shower, found the button, pushed it, eyes stinging with soap. Bumped someone.

"Quit shoving." Neil Tucker, right beside me.

"Yeah," said Branton, "somebody in here's been screwing Indians."

I tilted my face toward the shower head, washed the soap out of my eyes. Turned toward Branton just in time to see a naked Ivan Buchko stepping forward, like a giant emerging from a swamp, fog all around him. "Hey!" he said. "Enough. My turn for a shower." He nudged Branton with a massive hip, bumped him aside like someone knocking off a bug.

"Take it easy," said Branton. He glared at Ivan, uncertain what to think, then turned back at me. I could almost see him making up his mind. In the haze of steam behind him I noticed my brother come into the room, a bottle of shampoo balanced on his fingertip like a baton.

"No doubt about it," said Branton, "somebody around here's nothing but a squaw humper."

Blake grabbed him even before the shampoo hit the floor. Spun him around, drove him back, his head bouncing off the wall, Blake slamming him under the chin with a forearm, pinning him there. "Shut up," he said. "Shut your face — or I'll slap it shut." I was every bit as stunned as Branton, who couldn't have looked more surprised if he'd been sucker-punched by a priest in the middle of a prayer. All the guys who'd peeled away when Blake went for him were staring at them now. The only sound was water bouncing off the floor, spinning down the drain. I don't think Branton dared breathe with Blake still leaning into him, arm planted on his neck. Finally, Ivan Buchko stepped over, tapping Blake on the shoulder.

"You don't get in here pretty quick," he said, "hot water's gonna be all gone."

Ivan gave us both a ride home that night. When he pulled up in front of our house, he said to Blake, "If I was you, I wouldn't be calling any quarterback sneaks around the left end for a while. Don't think Branton'll be out there blocking for you." He laughed. "Man, he was shaking like a leaf. You hadn't had him pinned, he would've slid down the wall, disappeared right down the drain."

Blake snorted. It sounded like a cross between a laugh and a grunt. "He needs to watch his mouth."

We got out of the car, started around the side of the house, heading for the back door.

"You sure shut him up," I said. "Thanks." The sidewalk was narrow between the house and the fence, and Blake had stepped ahead of me, but as I spoke I reached out and gave his shoulder a quick squeeze. It was the first time we'd touched in ages.

He stopped walking, turned toward me, a puzzled look on his face. "What do you mean?"

I must have looked just as puzzled. "The way you handled him, I appreciate that. Bugger'd been giving me a rough time all afternoon."

"Shit," said Blake. "I thought he was riding me." He spun around, walked right by the backdoor and out to the picnic table under our crab apple tree. Sat down, his chin cradled in his hands. I glanced past him at the maple tree, the bird-feeder hanging crooked, but almost full, not a bird in sight. Surely, that damned hawk wasn't still around.

I followed Blake, slid onto the bench across from him, brushing a couple of withered crab apples out of the way. Blake didn't look at me. He was staring at a branch above my head, as if waiting to see when the last leaf would fall.

"He's been on me like a badger," I said. "What a prick." Blake was still studying the tree. "Why would you think he was riding you?"

My brother dropped his hands from beneath his chin. Finally looked at me.

"I figured he'd probably seen me — or someone might've told him."

"Told him what?"

"I took her out last night — Anna Big Sky."

I felt something rising in my throat, anger maybe, a flash of jealousy, I don't know, a surge of fear or craziness, something I'll never be able to explain, but I'd like to think that accounts for what happened next. "Those friends of yours," I said, "they get you all hot and bothered, going on about red meat?"

He hit me before I could move, a slap across the mouth, sudden pain, teeth jammed into my lip, the raw taste of blood. He grabbed me by the collar, twisting my shirt, yanking me toward him. "Don't! Don't ever say that."

I was choking, yeah, choking with shame. I'd just been repeating what they'd said, sure, but what a hell of a thing to say.

He held me inches from his face. I could almost feel the fire in his eyes.

"S-sorry. I didn't mean that."

I felt my collar loosening. He gave me a little push on the chest and released his grip.

I heaved a quick breath. Found myself straining for another. "Look, I apologize. Honest to God, I didn't mean that."

"Bloody well ought to apologize," he said, and I thought he sounded just like our father.

"I did. You heard me."

Except for a few leaves above us rattling in the breeze, the only sound was his breathing, gasps like those of a swimmer bursting into the air after he'd been underwater longer than he ought to be. I waited until his breathing calmed.

"What happened?" I asked.

"What do you mean — what happened?"

"When you took her out."

"Nothing happened." His voice was loud again. "We went for cokes — that's all."

He looked away, as if he had a secret he didn't want to share.

"Wait a minute. You're supposed to be grounded."

"I said I was working on my history project — at the library. And I was too — for a while. Had to be in by nine-thirty."

"Bet that impressed her." I made my voice as sarcastic as I could, but I couldn't leave it there. "You ask her out again?"

A crab apple fell on the table between us, misshapen, the colour of rust. He picked it up and tossed it to the ground.

"She said she didn't think it was such a great idea."

I was so filled with relief that I hardly noticed his voice sounding old and beaten, but then his expression darkened, his voice rising in volume: "She's interested though. You can always tell when they like you. I'm gonna try again."

Bullshit, I thought, you tried to cop a feel or something, and for the second time that day I said more than I should have. "You really figure she'd go out with a guy who pisses on girls?"

For just a second it was as if I'd hit him with a two-by-four. He shrank away from me, sinking lower into the bench. You'd swear he was smaller now, a blow-up toy that some kid had punctured, the air seeping out, and I thought I had him. His face at first was crimson, but the colour was already fading.

"Where did you hear that?"

"I was there. I saw the whole thing." He deserved to suffer. I'd make him suffer. "That poor girl, lying there unconscious. Could've choked on her own vomit — and died — for all you cared. And there you were, the bunch of you, lined up like you're standing over a bloody latrine."

He got his hands on the table, pushed himself up, hovered there above me, his face suddenly red again. "You got it wrong," he said, and he was yelling now. "I'm the guy who tried to stop them. They were all drunk out of their skulls — didn't know what they were doing — yeah, and I was drunk too, couldn't make them quit. But I wasn't pissing on her. That's the truth." He was staring down at me, as if by the sheer power of his gaze he could compel me to believe him.

"Like hell it is."

"Well, piss on you then," he said, and turned to go inside.

Five

We played the Weyburn Eagles that Saturday, a game we were expected to win. It had snowed on Friday night, five centimeters of snow followed by a few minutes of freezing rain. The field was coated with an icy crust. If we'd been playing in Regina at Mosaic Stadium there would have been a grounds crew to scrape it away, but we weren't the Roughriders so we played on snow and ice.

By the end of the first quarter, we were down fourteen to nothing. They had a running game that was hard to stop, their fullback a monster who seemed to enjoy running over people. Since he ran straight ahead and seldom made a cut, the snow didn't bother him. We knew he was going to get the ball a lot, but we couldn't seem to stop him, not without three or four guys on him, and by then he'd picked up six or seven yards. Our worst problem, though, was my brother. Twice he dropped the ball on the snap. His timing was off; he collided once with Vaughn Foster, our running back — almost knocked him over on the hand-off. He threw an early interception, and after that, he was overthrowing his receivers nearly all the time. When the offence came off, I watched him on the sidelines, receivers and backs around him, while Coach Ramsey drew a play on his chalkboard. Blake looked shell-shocked. He probably heard everything that Ramsey said, but I doubt that he understood a single word.

When the quarter ended and we switched ends, Coach Conley took him aside, the two of them walking down the field, far from where we stood. They had lots of time to talk because the Eagles were on the march again. I don't know what Coach said to him, but it must have been something special because by the time Blake came back to the rest of us, he looked different somehow, and I heard him yell, "Come on, defence. You can do it." The first encouragement I'd heard him give all afternoon.

Our guys were up against it now, on our three-yard line. The Eagles had one more down to score. In a situation like that most coaches would kick a field goal, but the Eagle coach had a fullback who could run through a brick wall. He wouldn't even consider it a gamble.

I could see our whole line crouched in the snow, could almost feel them vibrate with the tension, Ivan Buchko hunched low, waiting to hurl himself forward, Vaughn Foster poised behind him, Vaughn who only played defence when we were desperate. The ball was up, both lines surging forward. The handoff to the fullback, bodies straining, legs churning, Ivan breaking through, falling, an arm around the fullback's leg, Vaughn hitting the runner in the chest, two more of our guys on him, and he was going down. Stopped. A yard short of the goal. And on the sideline I was cheering, leaping up and down with everybody else.

My brother started onto the field, but Coach Conley stopped him, held him with a hand on his shoulder. "Nothing fancy," he said. "Up the gut till we're away from the goal line."

On the first play, Blake faded back to pass, faked it, saw the centre open up, and ran straight ahead a dozen yards, sliding safely to the snow before they had a chance to hit him. He hopped up, his arm raised for the huddle. He's back, I thought, we've got ourselves a football game. Blake stuck with the running game until we were nearing mid-field, then began working in short passes. Took us down to the twenty before running out of steam, Todd Branton dropping a pass he might've caught if he'd been a better player, and we had to settle for a field goal.

Okay, I thought, Blake's showed us how to do it. We can still win this game.

We did too, twenty-four to twenty-one, that one field goal making all the difference. Jordan Phelps scored twice on passes from my brother; Vaughn Foster got the other touchdown on a run, almost slipping on the ice as he cut over the goal line, but he stayed upright, the ball secure against his chest. I never got to play, but then I didn't expect to.

~~~

"How come he gets to go out?" I asked.

Blake had floated through supper, talking whenever his mouth wasn't full, laughing sometimes when there was nothing funny, eating way more than usual, still high from leading the come-back on that icy field. Then he'd said that Ivan was picking him up in half an hour, and I'd asked the question.

"His curfew's over," said my father. He noticed his fork in his hand, pointed it at me. "Yours isn't. Not till Monday."

"That isn't fair." I'd been grounded for nearly two weeks, and it seemed like forever. "He's the one who got drunk."

My father set his fork on his plate, sharply. It made a sound like a china bell that a grand lady might ring for dinner. Yeah, and we were into proper etiquette, weren't we though?

"Listen now. There's something here you need to understand. We don't condone drunkenness in this family; we just happen to think that fighting's worse. A lot worse. Is that understood?" My father was wearing his stern face, his eyes grim, unblinking, holding steady on me. I glanced away. Once again I cursed myself for lying about what had happened that night.

Blake was squirming in his chair, looking uncomfortable. The bugger, I thought, he knows how I got the shiner — Ivan must've told him.

"Blair!"

"Okay, okay! I understand."

My mother was leaning across the table, nodding her head.

Yeah, sure, fighting was serious business. I should tell them what went down before her father hit me, let them think about that for a while. Sure, Blake had said he didn't do it, but I figured the truth was he just couldn't admit it — especially to his little brother.

"Excuse me," he said. "I've got to get ready before Ivan's pounding on the door." He shoved his chair away from the table and hurried for the stairs. Yeah, and he'd probably be going to another party, getting sloppy drunk all over again.

I started to get up, changed my mind and settled back into my chair.

"I suppose the next thing we know," I said, "you'll want to be out looking for a fatted calf to kill."

My father laughed, but I was certain I detected a note of bitterness in the sound. "Different circumstances," he said. "'This son of mine was dead and is alive again' — somehow I don't think the case of the Prodigal Son applies in this instance. Uh-uh, no property squandered here in dissolute living."

You want dissolute living, I thought, well then, I could tell you a story would shake you to the core.

"If you're going to start spouting Biblical allusions," continued my father, "you ought to consider reading the Bible once in a while. I'd recommend chapter fifteen of Luke. Beginning at the eleventh verse. A little reading might open up your mind, maybe even knock it out of that rut you've got it stuck in."

By the time he finished speaking, his voice was sharp as the carving knife he always honed before he cut the turkey on Thanksgiving Sunday.

I couldn't tell him what I wanted to tell him. All I said was, "I'm going downstairs and watch the hockey game."

As I left the table, my father, who seldom quoted scripture outside the church, did what struck me as a remarkable thing. "Blair," he said, his voice assuming the exact tone he used when sharing the peace, "there's no need to be fighting everything. 'The Lord, your God, is in your midst, a warrior who gives victory; He will rejoice over you with gladness, He will renew you in His love.'"

I took the stairs two at a time.

⁓⁓⁓

Every Sunday after the service, my brother and I were expected to go down to the church hall for coffee with the congregation. It didn't matter that neither of us drank coffee. We were always stuck drinking watered-down Tang like the little kids from Sunday school. Usually, we sat together at a table off to the side, talking football and hoping that Mr. Hammond would join us with his take on the latest Rider game. He and his wife had season tickets. Today we'd barely sat down before Agnes Bettany headed for our table. She was slight and red-headed, bird-like in her manner, an older woman who hadn't aged a day since I'd been in kindergarten. My mother thought she didn't even dye her hair.

"Blair," said Mrs. Bettany, "you read so very well." It had been my turn to read the second lesson that morning, and I'd practiced at home as I always did, saying the whole thing out loud. "You put so much feeling into it, it really comes alive."

"Thank you, Mrs. Bettany. I work at it."

"Your father should have you read more often," she added before moving on to another table.

Blake watched her go, a sour look on his face. Uh-huh, I thought, he's remembering two years ago, when he was one of the readers for the Christmas Lessons and Carols and he screwed it up good, telling us about the wise men opening their treasure chests, offering gifts of gold, and myrrh and Frankenstein.

I thought I'd rub it in. "Nice of her to say so."

He turned blank eyes toward me. "Who?"

"Mrs. Bettany."

"What about her?"

"Oh, never mind. You might as well go back to sleep." He was hung-over again, that must be it.

I saw Mr. Hammond coming our way, coffee cup in one big hand, napkin and cookies in the other. Such a lean body, his hands so large, his voice so deep they always surprised me. He pulled a metal chair out from our table and sat down.

"Morning, boys," he said, and chuckled. "No, I guess it's after twelve. My brain is always running late. You make it into Regina for the game last night?"

I shook my head. "No, I had something else I had to do." Yeah, right, that would be staying at home by myself.

Blake was staring off again, in the direction of Mrs. Bettany.

"Too bad," said Mr. Hammond. "It was a good game even though they lost. Thirty-one to twenty-eight, lots of action up and down the field. Our guys gave it their best shot, but it's the same old problem. We need a quarterback you can count on — like Austin in his prime. Somebody like that throwing the ball, we'd really go places." He took a sip of coffee, seemed to be studying my brother. "Sorry I didn't make it to your game yesterday. Three hours in the cold is about as much as these old bones can handle in one day. I heard you won though."

When my brother didn't respond, I said, "Uh-huh, it was a close one too. Twenty-four to twenty-one."

"How'd you like playing in the snow, Blake?"

My brother moved his head as if a wasp had buzzed his cheek. "Pardon?"

"Here, have a cookie," said Mr. Hammond. "Maybe that'll snap you out of the coma."

I laughed. My brother just looked puzzled.

Mr. Hammond tried again. "How was it — in the snow?"

"Oh, it wasn't as tough as I thought it would be. Cold on the hands at first, but not bad once we got going." Blake's voice was dull, as if discussing a game that didn't much interest him. He had the words right, but the feeling wasn't there, his mood so different from his excitement last night at supper. "Defence won it for us. A big stand on the three-yard line."

Something's wrong, I thought, but what is it?

He didn't look hung-over, and as far as I knew he hadn't been throwing up last night. At least not at home where I would have heard him.

"You score any touchdowns?"

"Not me, no." The same dull voice, but then it changed. "Jordan Phelps, Vaughn Foster, they did the scoring." When he pronounced their names, his tone was sharper, the pitch of his voice higher. I'd never known him to be jealous of other people scoring. I wondered what this meant.

All at once Blake seemed to realize Mr. Hammond was staring at him. "The Riders," my brother asked, " how did they make out last night?"

Mr.Hammond turned to me. "I don't know, Blair," he said, "but I think you better keep an eye on your brother. He's slipping back into the coma. Either that, or he's got himself lost pondering the intricacies of your dad's sermon."

He was thinking about something all right, but it sure wasn't a sermon. I wondered what he'd been up to last night. What kind of trouble was he in now? There must have been something weird going on to make him act this way.

When our father drove the family home from church, Blake sat with me in the back seat, shoulder pressed against the far door, his face turned to the window. Outside, it had begun to snow, large flakes drifting down, hardly a breeze to disturb them as they floated in leisurely spirals like wisps of tissue, settling at last to cover the crust of snow from the day before. Only the middle of October and already our second fall of snow.

"Look at it," said my mother. "Around here, you seldom see it snow without a wind. Usually a howling wind. It's beautiful." She glanced back at Blake, but I don't think my brother was looking at the snow.

Before I went to bed that night I stood for a long time at my bedroom window. The snow had stopped falling hours ago, but the world outside was white and still, shining under the streetlights. When I switched off the light, the ceiling of my room seemed almost luminescent. I lay down and stared at the dim glow that had to be reflections from the snow outside.

For some reason, I thought of the time my brother took me Christmas shopping at Zellers. I was in grade three and he in grade six. He'd helped me pick out coffee mugs for our parents, nice ones with a Canadian flag on the side; then he left me in the line to pay for them. It was a long line, but I didn't care. I remember being pleased because the mugs weren't going to cost as much as I thought they would. I'd have money left over for a chocolate bar.

The next time I saw my brother, a man wearing a tie and vest had him by the arm, was almost dragging him along. They seemed to be arguing. When they got close to me, I heard Blake say, "That's him — in the green tuque. Just wait till he's paid. I don't want him getting lost."

What's he talking about, I thought, I'm way too big for getting lost.

The two of them stood there, watching me while the clerk rang up my purchases and counted out my change. They weren't arguing now. The clerk wrapped tissues around the mugs and slipped them into a bag. I handed her the looney she'd just given me and said, "I'd like a Crispy Crunch too."

"Come on, kid. We haven't got all day." The man sounded angry.

I shoved the bar into my pocket and grabbed my change. "What's going on?" I asked.

Blake shook his head at me. The man gave his arm a yank and headed toward the other end of the store.

I had to trot along beside them to keep up. "What is it?" I asked.

The man stopped so suddenly, his face so angry when he spun towards me that I ducked my head. I thought he was going to hit me. "Your brother," he said, "is a lousy thief."

When he got us to the office he phoned my father, told him his son had been caught shop-lifting a CD, he wasn't phoning the police this time, but if the boy ever tried it again, there'd be no second chance, the police would be handling the case for sure.

The man was still angry, his knuckles white on the phone, and I thought he really wished he had that hand around my brother's neck. Then he said something I'll never forget. "You're a minister, aren't you? What the hell do you teach these boys?"

Blake took a step toward him, his face crimson. For a second I thought he might kick the man in the shin, but he stopped after one step. "It won't happen again," he said, his voice so low I'm not sure the man heard him.

When the man was finished on the phone, he walked us to Zellers front door and held it open. "Get the hell out," he said, "and don't come back."

"I never did anything wrong," I said. "I can come — "

"Shut up!" said my brother, and he started across the parking lot.

I caught up to him and grabbed his arm. "I don't get it. Why would you — "

"I don't know." He was almost yelling. "Motley Crue — I don't even like them." He shook me off and started walking again.

"When we get home you're really gonna catch it."

He turned to glare at me. "You think I don't know that. Come on."

When we got to the bus stop on the far side of the mall lot, I stopped, but he kept walking.

"It'll pick us up right here," I said.

"You think I'm getting on that bus with all those bloody people, you're crazy."

There was no one at the stop but us. "What people?"

"People staring." He glanced back at me, but he never slowed his pace. "Hurry up. We're walking."

And we walked all the way home, nearly two klicks it was, the snow on the sidewalks crunching beneath our feet, the sky already darkening, Christmas lights glowing on trees and bushes, red rope-lights curled around the pillars of front porches, a few deer sculpted with wire and silhouetted in white lights as they fed on snow-covered lawns, a three-dimensional manger scene, the Christ Child wrapped in a real blanket and luminous in a box of straw, my brother dragging his feet the closer we got to home, signs of the Christmas spirit everywhere and nothing but grief awaiting him at home, for Blake had brought shame upon our family. I would have volunteered for a spanking if it would have eased my brother's mind.

When we got home, Blake was summoned to the den and I followed behind until my father shook his head at me and closed the door. I stood in the hall a moment, wondering how he would punish Blake. I should have known he wouldn't yell at my brother, but I was surprised by the restraint I noted in my father's voice, the words indistinct behind the door, a steady flow, low and murmurous, the tone as soothing as a massage on aching muscles.

~~~

I looked for Anna in the halls at school, tried to run into her, but I never saw her once, not even on Tuesday when I hung around outside her history class until everyone had left the room. Blake gave me a funny look when he came out and saw me standing by the fountain, but he never said a thing, and I sure wasn't going to ask him where she was.

I first heard the talk on Wednesday morning.

Hurrying down to my locker to switch books between classes, I passed two boys going up the stairs, their voices loud and animated.

"Not in town," one of them said. "Somewhere out in the country."

"Jesus. Who would do a thing like that?"

That was all I heard, but I had seen their faces, flushed, excited. I wondered why I felt uneasy.

I pushed through the crowd around the lockers, found my own, began to turn the dial on my combination lock. From behind me I heard someone say, "In a field somewhere. North of town."

"Dead, you mean?"

"Yeah, they said a body on the radio."

The lock was shaking in my hand. I tried to hold it steady and work the dial, but the numbers were all wrong.

"It wasn't that cold last night, was it?"

"I don't know. But frozen was what they said."

The numbers on my lock were blurry now. When I turned the dial, they seemed to shift. A girl had joined the group behind me, her voice high and troubled, almost screeching, but I didn't turn around.

"I heard it was a native — that's awful."

"Yeah, you don't expect it here in Palliser. Maybe in Regina."

"It's awful anywhere." The girl's voice again.

"They said she'd been beaten."

"She? You mean it was a girl?"

"According to the radio."

I quit fooling with my lock, let it fall against the metal door, stood there, my nose almost pressed against my locker, staring at its dented surface, a gun metal grey.

The girl behind me began to sob. I think I knew what she was going to say even before she spoke. "Anna," she said, "she hasn't been at school all week."

I had to get out of there. "Excuse me," I said, pushing between them, my head down, almost running, wanting just to get away, going back up the stairs, heading for the front door, but no, there were always kids outside, where could I go? The football room, there'd be no one in it now, not a soul, the football room, that was the place. I bumped a kid as I turned into the hallway by the gym, someone I hadn't seen, almost flattened him against the wall.

"Hey!" he said. It was Evan Morgan. I hardly recognized him. "You hear about that body? It might be someone from our school."

I grabbed him, gave him a shove along the hall. "No," I said, "no, it couldn't be." I didn't want him looking at my eyes. Pushing open the door to the football room, I ducked inside. Empty, thank God, it was empty.

The room was a blur. I could barely see where I was going, but I felt as if my body had been set on automatic pilot. My legs walked me across the room to my locker, turned me around, sat me down on the bench where I always sat. Where everybody sat.

"Red meat," Jordan Phelps had said, "good for the appetite."

I dropped my head into my hands. "Anna," I thought, "oh, Anna." I may have said her name aloud, I think maybe I did, and the next thing I knew, I was bawling like a baby.

By Thursday morning every kid at school knew that Anna Big Sky's body had been found in a field north of town. Even the teachers knew. On the radio, the T.V., announcers said that a farmer driving on a grid road had spotted the body in a field, but they kept saying no name had been released, the police were waiting for the next-of-kin to be notified. There was no announcement of her name until the news at suppertime that night, and by then the kids at school had already collected over a hundred dollars to buy flowers for her funeral.

I didn't want to hang around the school that day at noon hour, didn't want to have to listen to kids going on about someone most of them didn't even know. I asked Ivan Buchko if I could catch a lift home with him.

"Sure," he said, "if you don't mind going the long way around."

I hopped into the front seat beside him. He was so big I swear the whole car slanted toward his side of the road. I guess I noticed more about the car this time than I had the night we took Amber Saunders home. It was a '76 Ford LTD, with the front seat shoved back as far as it would go, but Ivan's huge body was rammed behind the wheel as if he was just some slightly bigger than normal guy who'd crammed himself into an old Volkswagen Beetle. Somehow it was comforting to ride with a guy so big and strong you knew that nobody could ever beat him up and dump him in a field.

Ivan didn't turn at Huston Way, but kept driving straight up Main Street. "Where you going first?" I asked.

"The old McCauley place."

"What's that?"

"Old homestead — well, a farmyard. Where the house and barn used to be. Just trees and bushes now. Not much else.

People sometimes go out there to drink." He looked grim. "That's where she got it."

"Anna?"

"Yeah, Anna Big Sky."

I felt like asking him to stop the car and let me out, I could walk home. But something kept me seated there, a sense of inevitability I guess you'd call it, a feeling that a chain of events had long ago been set in motion and now something more was going to happen, something I was meant to be a part of.

"How do you know where to go?" I finally asked.

"From the news. I recognized the place."

Ivan followed the highway that ran straight north of town till we reached a gravel crossroad and he turned east, going fast on the gravel, gravel and snow, the sound of the tires changing as soon as we left the pavement, a dismal wail. Flat prairie stretched ahead of us, and the occasional farm, outbuildings huddled under a thin, white shroud. After a few kilometres I saw the McCauley place ahead of us and knew what it was without Ivan saying a word. The yard was set back from the road the length of a city block, a line of Manitoba maples on either side of the yard, their trunks thick and dark even in the noonday sun. Most of the bigger branches were down, some of them split in two and dragging on the ground though still attached to the trunk, everywhere around them a snarl of broken limbs. Between the rows of Maples was a caragana hedge that looked as if it hadn't been trimmed in years, the branches wild and tangled, in places stretching a dozen feet into the air.

Ivan pulled onto the side road and stopped the car. From a fence-post right beside the car, a hawk rose into the air, wings beating for an instant, then falling still and silent as it glided toward the McCauley place. It was stupid as hell — I know it was — but I shuddered when I saw the hawk.

"There," said Ivan, and pointed at the field. Perhaps two dozen metres into the field, an irregular orange rectangle was painted on the snow, fluorescent orange. I'd been looking at the hawk and hadn't seen it. Spray paint, I thought. Ivan left the car running and we walked into the stubble field, the crust of snow snapping with every step we took, the sun above us almost lost in cloud now, our shadows like dim ghosts moving across the field. There were lines of footprints leading forward, and just as many going back the other way, then a mass of prints in a circle around the orange rectangle which was broken in places where someone had stepped. There were fewer prints inside the circle. We stopped before the paint, hesitant to take another step, as if this were sacred ground where no one dared trespass.

Blighted sunlight, wind beginning to rise, wisps of snow lifting, gathering on the flattened crust, sifting through broken stalks of wheat.

There, where she had lain.

"Poor Anna," said Ivan.

My eyes were damp. I felt myself moving backward, was afraid I'd start to run.

"Yeah, let's go." Ivan, too, had seen enough.

We hurried back to the car. I could feel my shoulders shaking inside my jacket and hoped he wouldn't notice.

I was still shivering in the warm car.

"Sure as hell," said Ivan, "they wouldn't have done it there."

"They?" My body jerked against the seat.

"Whoever — I don't know." He glowered at me. "Nobody's going to beat her up out there — where any car coming along would see them." He gestured toward the farm yard. "Behind those trees, that'll be the place."

He drove slowly along the narrow road, which was thick with weeds and grass, but not thick enough to prevent you from seeing that other cars had taken the same route. As we passed the caragana hedge, the car bounced beneath us.

"Ditch," said Ivan. "Somebody dug it right across the road to keep people out. Kids must've filled it in years ago."

Beyond the hedge the yard was full of swaying grass rising at least a metre above the snow, but here and there were tracks where cars had pulled off the road, patches where the grass was trampled down. High on the branch of a broken maple I thought I saw a shadow move. In one corner of the yard, a ring of snow-covered rocks marked an abandoned firepit. Near them, barely visible through the swaying grass, orange paint outlined an awkward circle.

Ivan swung his door open, got out of the car, swung the door shut again. I watched him step toward the circle. Wondered why I was just sitting here, watching him go. Finally, I dragged myself out of the car and followed him to the circle's edge. Here the grass was trampled, the crust of snow beaten down, but there was no sign of blood. From the edge of the circle, uneven footprints laid down a crooked trail through a break in the maples and out into the stubble field. The trail of someone staggering. Half a kilometre in the direction Anna had taken, smoke rose from the farmhouse she must have seen and tried to reach. Where the trail began, here in the heart of the circle, the snow was stained with urine.

Six

Tires on gravel, motor hum were the only sounds as Ivan drove us back to the highway. Once he looked at me, and I shoved my Kleenex back into my pocket. It was already soaked anyway. Once, too, he spoke: "She was going in the right direction. Damn, if only she'd kept going." After that we were both quiet. He had his thoughts, and I had mine.

I kept seeing that patch of yellow snow, kept thinking — I turned to Ivan. "Put on the radio, will you? This silence is driving me nuts."

He gave me a funny look, but he punched a button on the dash and the car was filled with sound. Some country singer wailing on about his friends in low places.

"Maybe we shouldn't have gone out there," Ivan said, "but I knew her, you know. Somehow it kind of seemed the thing to do. To see where it happened. As if I owed her that much."

"Uh-huh. I knew her too."

We bounced onto the highway and headed back to town. I noticed Ivan glance again at the dash.

"We're not going to have time to make it home for lunch," he said. "Sorry. Maybe we better grab something at McDonald's."

I was sorry too. "Okay, sure. Fine with me."

That much piss, there must have been a bunch of them. Had the bastards tried to rape her and she'd fought back — was that what had happened?

"We'll try the drive-through," said Ivan. "We can eat on the way back to school."

"Yeah. Whatever." I'd left my lunch on my locker shelf at school, hadn't even thought about it, just wanting to get away from the place, and then we'd gone to somewhere worse.

We clattered over the C.N. tracks on the edge of town, the tracks that seldom carried a train anymore, drove past the Canadian Tire Store, the A and W, turned in at McDonald's.

"You want a Big Mac?" Ivan asked.

"I guess so, sure."

She had fallen in the snow and they had stood around her.

"Anything to drink?"

"No, that's okay." I wasn't even sure that I could eat.

Ivan stopped at the speaker. A burst of static, a distant voice, and he was putting in our order.

All of them looking down at her, where she lay, crumpled in the snow, one of them suddenly hauling out his dick to piss, the others reluctant maybe, but one by one joining in. And I was sure I knew who they were.

"You can always tell when they like you," Blake had said. "I'm gonna try again."

∼∼∼

The trouble was I didn't know what to do. I needed to talk to my brother, but he ignored me at football practice after school that day. They were working on a play where he lateralled to Vaughn Foster in the flat, then ran downfield himself so that Vaughn could pass the ball to him. A surprise play that might score a touchdown in a pinch. Yeah, and any kind of touchdown seemed like small potatoes now.

Football practice was no time for the kind of conversation I needed with my brother. I'd catch him at home.

When I went down for supper that night, there were only three places set at the table. My mother was busy at the counter, pouring soup into the frying pan.

"What's going on?" I asked.

She shot me a puzzled look before picking up a spatula and beginning to stir. "Just making Sloppy Joes is all."

"No." I pointed to the table. "Who isn't coming home for supper?"

She laughed. "Here, I thought I'd thrown you for a loop, putting soup in the fry pan. Your brother's sleeping over at Fosters."

"On a school night?"

"They've got that joint history project. Going to try to finish it tonight."

"Oh," I said. "Oh." But I knew history wasn't what they'd be discussing. They were up to something.

～～～

Standing in the hallway outside my father's den, I could see his left elbow on his desk and beside it the stack of books that he always kept at hand: *Cruden's Complete Concordance, The Concise Concordance, The New Compact Bible Dictionary* (the only paperback in the pile), *The New Oxford Annotated Bible, The Book of Alternative Services* (the B.A.S. he always called it). In front of them was a pile of loose papers weighted down with an Indian hammerhead he'd found years ago in the Coteau hills west of town. Beyond the papers and the books, I could see the dull glow of his powerbook. Until six months ago, a huge old computer had stood like a stone monument at the centre of his desk, but then he'd bought a laptop that he could cart back and forth to church. The best thing he'd ever done, he claimed, grinning as if he'd just won the lottery. It didn't take much to make him happy.

I knew he must be working on his sermon, but I needed to talk.

When I stepped into the den, I could hear his fingers tapping the keys, but barely, for his touch was light and quick.

"You got a minute?"

Half a dozen words marched across the screen, followed by a period. He turned in his swivel chair. "Sure. Have a seat." He smiled at me, that warm smile that said he didn't mind the interruption, and I thought, he's a good person, he can help if anybody can.

He motioned to the straight chair beside his desk. "Just set the minutes on the floor."

I moved the binder of vestry minutes from the chair to the floor and sat down. A couple of pages must have been loose in the binder; they had partially slid onto the floor, white paper stark against the dark hardwood of the den. Like snow on rock, I thought.

"Well?"

You'd think I would have figured out what I was going to say. I'd tried, running things over in my mind, looking for ways of coming at the problem indirectly, of getting my father's advice without his ever knowing what it was I had to ask him about, but nothing seemed to make any sense. I was going to have to launch into something and see where it took us.

"There's this kid at school," I said.

He was leaning forward in his chair, his hands on his knees. "Yes?"

"He's got this problem, and he doesn't know what to do."

My father sat back in his chair, his expression thoughtful. "But he's got a problem and he wants you to help him with it?"

"Uh-huh, he came to me." What could I say that wasn't going to sound stupid? "I guess he knew I was a preacher's kid. Thought I might be the one to tell him what to do."

"Well, son, you might suggest he get down on his knees and try a prayer." Sheesh! That was going to be a big help. For just an instant though I thought I saw a flash of merriment in his eyes, but I must have been mistaken, for he had more to say. "When I'm in a quandary about something, whenever I feel lost and don't know what to do, when there's a problem I just can't get a handle on, well, that's the time I go into a quiet room and take it to the Lord. It doesn't always help, you know, but sometimes it does."

I grabbed *The Book of Alternative Services* from the stack on his desk, its cover a rich, dark green, the feel like leather. I ruffled its pages with my thumb. "The thing is, this kid, I don't think he's religious."

"I see." My father studied me, his right hand rising to his ear, his index finger stretching out to touch it. He had a habit of tracing the outline of his ear with his finger whenever he was lost in thought, and I knew he was thinking now. "There was that girl from your school whose body they found." He almost caught me with that, but I was sure I hadn't flinched. "The native girl we talked about. Would this have anything to do with her?"

"No, of course not." Was I protesting too much? "At least, I don't think so."

He was still fingering his ear. "Did this kid say what his problem was?"

"Not exactly." I knew I was floundering.

"Yet he expects you to help him solve it?"

"I guess so. Yeah."

My father leaned forward in his chair, the swivel creaking beneath him. He reached out and patted my knee. "He makes it difficult, not giving us anything to work with. What exactly did he say?"

I never pray at bedtime anymore, but I prayed then. Oh, Lord, please, find some way to get me through this conversation.

"He said he had a friend, and this friend had done something pretty stupid, something they both knew was wrong. Only his friend didn't know he knew. But he knew all right — the first kid — and he had to decide what to do. Whether to tell him — or turn him in." I sucked in a breath of air. "He couldn't very well just keep quiet. It wouldn't be right."

"No, I guess it wouldn't."

My father stared at me, and I stared back at him. Way down in the basement I heard the furnace come on, felt the pipes vibrate, the air begin to stir around us.

"Look, Blair," my father said, "this kid must have told you something more. Something specific. What exactly did he say?"

"Nothing, really. He just seemed . . . well, troubled."

"Come on, son. You've got to talk to me. What's going on here?"

"That's it. That's all I know."

"Uh-huh." Two syllables, and I knew he was angry. I had to say something.

"The thing is . . . he thought that you — that I — might tell him what to do."

"Well, Blair," he said, his voice calmer now, "I suppose he could try talking to his friend. Maybe they can work things out between them." For a second he looked as if he might swing around in his chair, go back to work on his computer, but he was only shifting in his seat. "From the little bit you've told me, I'd have to say this kid at school has a pretty good idea of right and wrong. I think he already knows what to do. Maybe he just needs somebody to tell him to go ahead and do it."

"I guess so, yeah, you're probably right." I stood up, took a step towards the door, remembered the vestry minutes on the floor, scooped them up and set them back on the chair. When I was almost out the door, my father spoke again.

"Be strong," he said, "and let your heart take courage."

"What's that?" I hesitated, but I didn't turn around.

"A line from the Psalms. Many people find some comfort there." I heard a slight sound behind me, like someone in the audience at a tense drama quietly clearing his throat. "But then," he continued, "I guess you said this kid wasn't religious, didn't you?"

"That's right, yeah." I hurried down the hall toward my own room.

～～～

I lay awake for hours, thinking about my brother and the way he'd changed until I hardly knew him anymore, his strange behaviour Sunday morning, and before that his certainty that she'd go out with him, eventually she would, and now she was dead and he was off somewhere with Vaughn Foster, the two of them going over everything that had happened, and not just the two of them either, Jordan Phelps, he was the one who said she needed a good banging. And Phelps had called her bitch. Anna Big Sky, who'd found him with Amber Saunders pinned against the lockers and she hadn't hesitated, hadn't worried about herself, stepping in where she was needed, setting Amber free, doing what she knew she had to do, then walking by me, eyes on fire, you could see them burn, and she was right, she was, doing what she did.

Anna walking down the hall, other times, head up, high cheekbones, the severe line of her mouth, walking toward me, "Blair," she'd say, "Blair," her mouth relaxing into that sudden smile that made her beautiful, and I could hardly breathe.

Anna striding down the hall, teachers nodding at her, Mr. Helsel smiling because she was someone special, Anna marching out the door, tramping through the snow, and there they were, a line of guys, in the shadow of the broken trees, and Mr. Helsel was laughing now, but it wasn't Mr. Helsel, it was just a skull, fractured teeth laughing, and Jordan Phelps was there, Jordan and my brother, groping for their flies, but she was past them now, reaching for a door, she was going to get away, but it wasn't a door, it was a lid, a coffin lid, she was lying in a coffin, and the lid was falling shut.

Quick, shallow breaths, and I knew that they were mine. The red glow like a warning from my clock radio. Nearly one o'clock in the morning.

I'd fallen asleep after all.

I flung my covers off and headed to the bathroom for a drink, but when I switched on the bathroom light I saw that the door to my parents' room was open. I tiptoed to the head of the stairs, taking care to skirt the squeaky board. I wondered if my father was down there telling my mother about the strange conversation he'd had with me that evening.

The floor below was dark, but I could see a faint light down the hall by the kitchen, where they often sat over hot chocolates, discussing the events of the day before they went to bed. They seldom stayed up late.

With my hand on the banister, I stood poised and listening.

Steady purring from the furnace, curtains whispering at my parents' open window, occasional creaking as pipes expanded, the house shifting in the cool night air. Nothing audible from the kitchen.

I considered creeping down the stairs, but there were six noisy steps in a row, and I was sure that they would hear me. I got my glass of water and went back to bed.

~·~·~

I knew my brother would be in the student lounge at noon. Its tables were reserved at lunch hour for students in grades eleven and twelve; the nines and tens were assigned to the basement where two separate classrooms were designated lunchrooms.

Eating lunch in room 110 was different now. Normally, there'd be someone at the door keeping an eye out for the teacher on noon duty, and six or eight kids tossing crumpled lunch bags back and forth, maybe a game developing, two sides forming, everybody trying to lob a bag against the wall where no one from the other side could catch it. I sat in the desk beside Evan Morgan who looked as glum as I felt. "School's crawling with counsellors," he said. "They're talking to all the grade twelves."

"Yeah, grief counsellors, I know." But I didn't want to think about it. As soon as I finished my lunch, I said, "Got an errand to run. I'll see you in class."

I walked up the stairs and past the school entrance to where the hallway opened into the lounge. Most of the chairs were full of kids, nobody laughing or joking around today, most of them talking quietly or just sitting, staring out the windows, a table tennis game going on over by the coke machine, but you could tell nobody cared who won. There was a girl in the corner yapping on a cell phone, but when she noticed me staring at her, she looked embarrassed and dropped her voice. No sign of my brother. Some of the football players were leaning on the sill beneath the windows, but he wasn't with them. Then I saw him sitting on a metal chair beside the glass trophy case that separated the lounge from the hall. I waved at him, but he didn't see me. If I went into the lounge at this time of day, I knew that someone was bound to tell me that it was off-limits, that snot-nosed freshies should get back where they belonged, into the basement.

I walked along the hallway, watching him through the trophy case. The double sheets of glass made him look distorted, but I could see that he was by himself, sitting off to the side, away from the tables which were all packed with eating kids. When I was abreast of him, I noticed the trophy in the case between us, a bronze football player, ball tucked beneath his arm, one leg in the air but looking rather awkward and not quite in sync with the other leg, which was attached to a rectangular wooden base with a plaque upon it. The George Reed Most Valuable Player Award. I knew without reading the names on the plaque that last year, for the first time ever, the award had gone to somebody in grade eleven, Jordan Phelps.

I stepped away from the trophy to get a better view of Blake. He was gnawing on a chocolate bar, a Coke can and a couple of empty cheesie bags on the table beside him. I guess Mrs. Foster hadn't made him lunch.

I tapped on the glass. Gave it a good rap when he didn't turn around. And another.

Finally, he heard the noise and slowly turned, no change of expression when he looked up and saw that it was me. If I hadn't known better, I might have thought he knew all along that I was there.

I motioned with my hand for him to follow me. "Come on," I said, just mouthing the words. I pointed at myself and then at him. "I need you. Come on."

He gave me a look that was void of expression, then bent over, hoisted his drink to his lips, finished it with three long pulls, slowly closed his hand, crushing the can, and pitched it into the recycle barrel. He bent down once more, picked up the empty bags, rolled them together into a ball with the wrapper from his bar, and, as he started walking by the trophy case, dropped his paper ball into the garbage can.

I walked beside him, holding myself back, strolling as he was strolling, the case like a wall between us till it ended near the gym. For some crazy reason, I thought of that poem I'd read in my brother's English text, the one with the weird line: "Good fences make good neighbours." And what would fences do for brothers, I wondered, but by then he was facing me.

"What do you want?"

"We need to talk."

"So? Talk."

"This isn't a good place."

"Seems good enough to me." He was being difficult.

"At least come down the hall where no one's going to hear."

He pointed behind me, back the way that I had come. The entrance was full of kids, some of them pushing into the lounge, others congregating by the washrooms.

"I meant the other way," I said. "By the gym."

He turned without another word and walked down the gym hallway. It was empty and he went only part way toward the coaches' office, stopping by the oak wall-hanging that someone had once made in woodwork class, the one that extolled the virtues of sportsmanship, the message scorched into the oak with a wood-burning kit.

"Okay, no one's going to hear a thing. What do you want?"

Now that he was ready to listen, I didn't know how to say it. His eyes were grey and cold, like dirty ice. I glanced at the wall-hanging over his shoulder. "Athletic ability," it said, "and strength of character." Was there any correlation left between them, I wondered. Had there ever been?

"Come on." His words quick and impatient.

"Yeah, okay, but if it wasn't you I wouldn't say a thing. It's just that . . . well, you're my brother." I took a deep breath. I had to get it out. "I know what happened."

"What the hell are you talking about?"

"I was out there — north of town — where she died. Ivan drove me out."

"Ivan." His voice was quiet, but I thought he looked surprised.

"Yeah, and I'm not just talking about that field where they found her. We took the dirt road into the McCauley place, back through the trees. Saw the patch of ground where they beat her." I couldn't make myself say, "Where you beat her," but I could see that he was troubled now. He was barely breathing. "I know what happened to her." Okay, spit it out. "I know who was there."

He gave his head a violent shake. "You don't know squat."

"Listen, I'm trying to help you here. I'm — "

"You keep your mouth shut. Understand?"

"No. I'm going to the cops. It's the right thing to do." He was glaring at me, and I felt my temper rising. "Nobody deserves to die like Anna did — beaten up till she can hardly walk, cold and scared and covered in piss. I don't know how you could — " I stopped, tried to get control. "This is how it's got to be. After school tonight I'm going to tell the cops, but you can do it first. I want you to have a chance. If you come clean, maybe then — "

"You want *me* to have a chance?" He leaned back against the wall and laughed, his laugh bitter as acid. He reached for me then, grabbed me by the shoulders and thrust me hard against the wall. Shoved his face into mine. "You haven't got a clue how it happened," he said. "Not a single clue. So you can forget about squealing to the cops. I'm the one who's gonna work this out, and you can just shut the hell up." He released his grip on my shoulders, looked as if he might say something more, but instead turned and walked away.

He'd had me rammed against the wall, his breath hot in my face, and now I realized his spittle was on my chin. I wiped it off with the back of my hand, almost expected to feel acid burns on my skin.

Seven

We were reading the one act play *Summer Comes to the Diamond O* in class that afternoon, a goofy cowboy comedy was what Miss Lambert said it was, something we could have some fun with. There were grief counsellors talking to the senior grades, sure, but they probably figured those of us in grade nine were so far removed from Anna Big Sky that carrying on like normal was the best thing for us to do. Of course, we were expected to volunteer for all the parts in the play, those with the main roles pulling their desks to the front of the room and turning them around so they could face the rest of us as they read. I didn't volunteer for anything. I'm not exactly sure what the play was about, a bunch of cowhands coming in for dinner in a cookshack, something about a stranger who tells them fancy stories, but I kept drifting off to things that really mattered.

I wondered what I ought to do. If only my brother wasn't involved — that complicated everything. It would've been easy to turn Jordan and the rest of them in, but my brother — that was different. Why the hell couldn't he just this once have done what I asked him? But oh no, he wanted me to stay out of it. As if there was any way he could handle it himself. He didn't give a damn about Anna, didn't care about anybody but himself. Never had.

No, that wasn't fair.

He didn't used to be like that.

The stranger going on about real old-fashioned baking powder biscuits, how nice and firm they were, and suddenly I was somewhere else, with my brother, out at Douglas Park, the two of us gazing across the beach at the grey waters of Diefenbaker Lake, white caps rolling into shore, kids on air mattresses laughing and hooting, riding the waves like cowboys, and neither one of us could swim. I was maybe four at the time. "Listen now," my father said. "You two stay right here on this blanket. I just have to run up to the washroom. Be back in a minute." As soon as he was out of sight around the corner of the washroom, I headed for the water.

"You're s'posed to stay here," said Blake.

"I'm just gonna wade a bit. Up to my ankles."

The water wasn't even cold. The bottom was all sand under my feet, not a rock anywhere, the sand in lines of little ridges where the waves washed it in. You could scratch them with your toes or stomp them with your heels, and the water got all fuzzy with sand.

There was a kid on a yellow sea-horse, a little kid, not much bigger than me, it was bucking in the waves and he kept falling off and grabbing it, climbing on to ride again, but I knew that it would get away from him, pretty soon it would, and then I'd have my chance, I'd grab it and show him how to ride. He was off again, a big wave lifting it, heaving it away, and now I was gonna show him, but my feet went down.

The bottom wasn't there.

Somehow the water got on top of me.

I could just see that yellow sea-horse up above, rolling up above, but I couldn't get to it, and I was rolling too. I tried to yell, but there was water in my mouth, I was coughing, spitting and coughing, more water coming in. Something underneath my arms, lifting, my mouth was in the air, coughing, choking, it was Blake had a hold of me, only he was going down, and so was I, but I had a mouth full of air, and he was right beside me, I could see him in a blur of water shaking, splashing, bubbles streaming from his nose, and I needed up again, I got my hands on his shoulders, tried to push myself up, if I could only get my head above the water. . .

My father's face like a fish before me, a few strands of hair streaming off his head, seaweed in the current, and he had me around the waist, lifting, and my head was out of the water, I was breathing air, and Blake was right beside me, he'd be breathing too, our father dragging both of us back toward the beach, setting us down on the sand, kneeling in front of us while we gasped and coughed.

I'd expected him to give me heck, to turn me over his knee and nail me with the spanking I deserved, but he never even yelled. His voice was just a whisper when he spoke. "Blair," he said, "Blair, you could have drowned." When I was through coughing, he put a hand on either side of my face and held me still, his head lowered to my own. "Listen now. You must never go in the water unless I'm there, or your mother is. Right there. You understand?" His grip on my face was so tight I could barely nod my head. "Good. That's important. I hate to think what would have happened here if it wasn't for your brother." He let me go then and turned to Blake, but I could still feel his fingers on my cheekbones.

"Blake, I know you were trying to help, going in after him like that. But you can't swim, it could've been the end of you too. You were very brave, son, but you should have called an adult." He said some more, his voice quiet, still surprisingly calm, I guess, but I was crying by then and didn't hear the rest. Blake was crying too.

I found myself rubbing my eyes, and all around me kids were snickering. I scrunched down in my seat, but it was okay, they were laughing at the play. A sheriff had walked into the cookshack and called the stranger Windy. "Windy!" someone exclaimed, and the kids reading at the front were all trying to look horrified.

He was my brother, and he used to be a good guy. How was I going to turn him in? If he hadn't been drinking, this never would've happened — I knew that was the truth. It was the beer, it had to be.

Yeah, but it did happen. Anna was dead. They'd already shipped her body back to the reserve at Wood Mountain, and there was going to be a big funeral early next week. I wanted to go, but I wasn't sure my parents would let me out of school. When the funeral was out of town like that — not in Wood Mountain, but in Assiniboia, which was almost as far away — hardly anybody from school would be there, well, maybe the girls' volleyball team and a few close friends, and somebody sent to represent the student council. She deserved more than that.

Uh-huh, she deserved justice. But for her it was too late for that. The guys who did it to her, though, they needed to see how justice worked. It would have been easy, too, if it was just Jordan Phelps, Jordan and Vaughn Foster, sure, and Todd Branton, but this was Blake, my brother, I wasn't sure that I could do it. Except I knew it was the right thing to do.

"This kid at school," my father had said, sounding almost as though he knew who the kid was, "has a pretty good idea of right and wrong. I think he already knows what to do." And maybe he did figure out that I was the kid. Because then he had to go and quote the Bible: "Let your heart take courage."

As if that was going to help me.

And this Windy fellow was yapping on about the time he sailed around Cape Horn and he was sleeping in a hammock while the ship ploughed through huge waves, and the kids playing parts and the others in their desks, they were all listening to him just as if his name wasn't Windy and he wasn't full of crap.

~~~

I knew I'd be late for practice after school that day. The telephone was in the hall by the gym where kids were always using it to phone home for rides after games and practices. Kids like me who didn't have cell phones. Some days you'd look down there and there'd be such a line-up, sheesh, you'd think the school had a bloody ban on cell phones. The halls would take a while to clear after the bell at 3:30, and I sure as heck didn't want anyone hearing what I had to say. I stayed at my desk, working on the questions we'd been assigned in English class, but they didn't make much sense because I'd been in such a haze throughout the reading of the play. At 3:45 I gave it up, dumped my books into my locker and headed for the gym.

The hall was empty except for one guy, Al Richardson, and he was on the phone. One of the debate team, he was the kind of person who hated silence as much as any deejay blathering between programmed selections on the radio. I walked past him, into the lounge and got myself a coke from the drink machine.

Moment of panic. I plunged my finger back into the coin pocket on my jeans. No, it was okay, I still had money for the phone.

I pulled a chair over to where I could watch Richardson and went to work on my coke. One hand held the phone beside his ear, of course, but the other hand, his right one, was slicing patterns in the air, beating out the rhythm of his words. Man, all I'd have to do is tie down that hand and he'd totally lose his ability to speak — he'd have to hang up the phone. Come on, I thought, get it over with. He paused once for what must have been a full minute, his right hand hanging lifeless at his side. He was leaning against the wall now, turning back and forth, almost writhing, listening to whoever was on the other end of the line, the pain of keeping silent too much for him. Twice I saw his mouth open, then fall shut again, disappointment like a mask on his face. Another second and he made his move, lips flapping, his right hand back in action. Yeah, he came off that wall like a player coming off the bench when the coach sends him into the game with a trick play they know is going to mean their last chance to win.

I dropped my empty can into the bin and ambled down toward him. Maybe if I hung around beside the phone he'd take the hint.

I was almost upon him when his eyes seemed to focus on me, as if he suddenly realized this object coming towards him wasn't just a piece of moving furniture, and he turned away from me, hunching over, shielding the phone with his shoulder. Probably trying to impress some girl, I thought. The jerk likes himself almost as much as Jordan Phelps. I walked past him so he couldn't pretend I wasn't there, and leaned against the wall a few yards from him. He immediately turned the other way, cupping his right hand over his mouth and the phone to cut down any chance that I might hear whatever line he was using. Hey, maybe that would do the trick. He was going to have trouble keeping up his share of the dialogue with his hand motionless beside his mouth.

I pulled out a quarter, began to flip it into the air and catch it. After another minute he glanced over his shoulder.

"You gonna be long?" I asked.

"I paid my money," he said. "Don't rush me." But his voice was quiet on the phone, his hand still, the animation gone from his chatter. I had him now. It was just a matter of time.

After yet another minute, I heard him say, "I got to go now. There's some creep here keeps trying to listen in." When he hung up the phone, he stuck his nose in the air and walked past me without another word. Yeah, but if he'd been Jordan Phelps, he would've body-checked me into the wall. I waited until he had gone all the way down the hall and disappeared toward the outside door.

I couldn't just phone 9-1-1, could I? This wasn't exactly an emergency, not now it wasn't, and back on Saturday night, when someone might have saved Anna, nobody was phoning the police to help her. I grabbed the directory from where it was chained in the rack beneath the phone. "Crime Stoppers," that was what they said on T.V. They were always doing robbery re-enactments on the suppertime news, guys wearing ski masks sidling toward cash registers in convenience stores, pulling knives, threatening clerks, running outside with handfuls of cash, a policeman in full close-up abruptly commandeering the screen to tell us about the importance of phoning Crime Stoppers if we had any information that might in any way be useful. Oh man, I could tell him what he needed to know.

My hands unsteady, I flipped through the yellow pages. "CRESTS," "CRISIS CENTRES," but no headings between them. Jeez, you had to be a sleuth just to find the damned phone number. I tried the white pages, some names in huge bold print and highlighted in yellow, some in smaller bold print, "CRESTVIEW ROOFING LTD" leaping out at me, and "CROCKER DAVID CHARTERED ACCOUNTANT", and nothing but small print between them. Didn't these guys want your tips?

But there it was, in the small print, "Crime Stoppers (Saskatchewan)" and an 800 number (Call No Charge). I checked both ways down the hall. Not another person anywhere in sight. No charge — did that mean for pay phones or long distance? I dropped my quarter in the slot just in case and pressed the numbers: 1-800-222-8477, and almost dropped the phone when a girl was immediately on the line, not a single ring at her end, but there she was, talking to me: "Thank you for calling the Crime Stoppers Tip Line." Just a recording, I thought, she isn't really there, this might be okay. "Your help is appreciated, and we want to assure you that at no time will your call be monitored or traced. To reach Palliser Crime Stoppers, press One. To reach Saskatchewan Crime Stoppers — "

I pressed one.

This was it then; I was going to do it. *Brnnng . . . Brnnng . . . Brnnng . . .* four . . . five . . . six rings — they didn't give a damn — seven rings, and someone was picking up the phone. "Hello. Crime Stoppers." A woman's voice. "How can we help you?" This was a real woman on the other end of the line, I could hear her breathing, she was waiting for me to talk. "Can I help you?" An edge to her tone.

"Yes." Damn, my voice like a squeak, but I could lower it. I took a deep breath. "I want to report a crime." No, that wasn't right. They knew about the crime. "Report *on* a crime. This girl from school, Anna Big Sky, she was killed. The cops — " no, they wouldn't like me saying 'cops' " — the police, they already know that, but I can tell them who did it." I'd hardly said a thing, yet I was out of breath, almost gasping.

"I'm going to give you a number, sir." She was all politeness now. "It will protect your identity, but you'll still be eligible — "

"I don't want a bloody number."

"Go ahead, then." She was still trying for politeness, but her voice was curt. "If you can give me names, that would be helpful."

I could still hang up.

Just drop the phone on the cradle and walk away from here, hustle down to the locker room and get dressed for practice, everything would be okay, nobody would guess what I'd nearly done. Blake would never know.

Yeah, but I had a pretty good idea of right and wrong — my father knew that much, didn't he? — and what they'd done was wrong.

"Jordan Phelps," I said. "He'd be the one who got them started. Todd Branton, you can bet that he was there, and . . . Vaughn Foster — probably him too. Those guys — they do everything Phelps says." The light above my head was flickering. I looked up, one fluorescent tube going on and off and on again, as if it couldn't make up its mind about what it ought to do. "I don't know how many were involved all together, but those three, they're the guys to check. Have the police talk to them."

And one other guy, I thought, Blake Russell, but oh no, I couldn't say his name. Did it matter though? The rest of them would be quick to turn him in.

She read the three names back to me and added, "Now, you're sure about this information?"

"Yes," I said, "but I wish I wasn't," and I hung up the phone.

I thought I'd feel better after I made the call, but somehow I felt worse.

~·~·~

After I got into my equipment, I sat for a long time on the bench, staring into my locker, my jeans hanging in the shadows like a haggard outlaw dangling from a gallows. What about Blake, what was going to happen there? They'd get him anyway, I thought, even though I chickened out and didn't say his name. Finally, I kicked the locker door shut and left the room.

My brother was on the practice field, working out of the shotgun because our centre needed to practice his long snaps. Blake was throwing passes to five different receivers, but they were dogging it, trotting through their routes, laughing and waving at balls they should have been catching, horsing around, I guess, while Coach Conley was down by the goal line, working with the other linemen. When I trotted onto the field, I couldn't see Blake's eyes because of the dark visor on his helmet, but I could tell from the thrust of his jaw that he was angry. If I was a receiver, I'd be running full-out every time he threw the ball. I looked around for Jordan Phelps — he never dogged it when a pass was thrown his way — but there was no sign of him. No sign of Vaughn Foster either.

I tried to keep a blank look on my face, but it wouldn't matter — he could always read me like an actor with a script.

When Blake saw me coming he was fading back to throw, but he stopped, his arm cocked, and studied me, his jaw thrust out even farther. I knew what he was thinking. Yeah, one look and he knew. He took a step toward me.

"Shit," he said, "shit! You've gone and done it." He hurled the ball at my head, but I got my hand up in time to knock it away. He wrenched his helmet off, glaring at me, and I prepared to duck, but he stood there for a long moment, his body rigid, motionless. In the end he fired his helmet at the goalpost. When it hit, there was a sharp crack, which must have been the visor breaking, and the helmet bounced to the ground. Before it stopped rolling, my brother had walked off the field.

On his way toward the gate, he strode past Coach Ramsey, who was usually late for practice after getting off work at the asphalt plant. Blake went by him so close, in fact, that he almost bumped him. Ramsey stopped and said something — I could see his lips move, but I couldn't hear what he said. Whatever it was, it had little effect on Blake; he spoke to Ramsey, a word or two, but he kept right on walking toward the door of the gym.

When Ramsey turned around, he looked flustered and hurried onto the field. He noticed me watching him and came directly towards me.

"What the hell's wrong with Blake?"

I shrugged.

He reached for me then, tapped me on the chest, his finger like a spike. "I saw him throw that ball at you. Then he says, 'My stupid brother told.' What the hell's going on?"

"He's pissed off at me, I guess." I almost shrugged again, but caught myself in time. "He's pissed off a lot lately."

"*He's* pissed off? You want to see pissed off, watch me if he doesn't get the hell back out here. And soon too." He put his hand flat on my chest, pushed me back from him. Took a step away, then swung around again. "Trouble with your brother, he's got a swelled head. Just because he's throwing to the best receiver this league ever saw, he thinks he's a half-assed quarterback."

"He's a good quarterback."

Ramsey was so close I could feel his breath on my face. For a second I thought he was going to take a swing at me, his right hand coming up fast, but it hovered in front of me, one finger extended, pointing beyond my shoulder.

"Get the hell out there and run your laps," he said.

I wasn't crazy enough to argue with him. I turned and jogged toward the track that circled the field.

～～～

"Where's your brother?" my father asked. We were at the supper table, chicken noodle soup and toasted cheese sandwiches laid out before us.

I shook my head. "He's not upstairs." I took a bite of the sandwich, felt the melted cheese hot on my lower lip. The little television was on, the suppertime news coming at us from the far corner of the kitchen counter. When the weather man stepped before his map, my father picked up the remote and turned the volume down a few notches. The guy was always laughing at things that weren't funny, his laugh loud and phoney.

My mother had her spoon in her soup, was idly stirring it in little circles. "I don't know what's with him lately," she said. For a second, I thought she meant the weather man. "He hasn't been himself all week. There's something on his mind."

"He's been pretty slack about his homework too," said my father. "Maybe needs some tuning up."

The poor bugger, I thought, Jordan would've ratted on him, he's probably getting tuned up right now. I could picture him in some bare room in the basement of the police station, a couple of tin chairs, a single wooden table, somebody leaning across the table, grilling him, shaking a nightstick in his face, my brother squirming on the chair, another cop pacing behind him, nodding, yes, that's the idea, another minute and he's going to break.

"Anything at school? Blair?" My father was staring at me, a puzzled expression on his face.

"Pardon?"

"I was talking to you. Maybe Blake isn't the only one who needs some tuning up." His voice was louder than before, but he looked frustrated rather than angry.

"I was trying to catch the forecast."

"And I was asking if you'd noticed anything at school — about your brother."

There was no way I could tell them what I knew. "He doesn't talk to me all that much anymore." I took a bite of my sandwich, the cheese cooler now. My father waited while I chewed.

"Something going on between the two of you?"

"I don't know — not really." They'd find out soon enough, but someone else would have to tell them. Still, I had to say something. "Being quarterback, I think maybe all that responsibility is getting to him. And Coach Ramsey's a bit of a dink."

"Blair!" My mother's interjection.

"Coach Conley's in charge, isn't he?" My father again. He said something more about the coaching, but I was watching the television, Anna Big Sky's face in black and white, a yearbook photograph was what it was, that smile frozen there, the same smile she wore whenever we passed in the halls, a photo the only way anyone would see it now or ever again, the volume still turned down low, but in the silence after my father's words, I heard the announcer say there was breaking news, the police were expecting to make arrests, of high school boys, no names would be released.

"You know anything about this?" my father asked.

I shook my head, wishing I hadn't been so busy staring at the television set that I'd missed the reaction of my parents. I wondered, did they have any suspicions?

EIGHT

When the doorbell rang, I was in my room, staring at my geometry text, a series of triangles that kept shifting beneath my gaze. I went to the window, pulled the curtain aside and looked down on a police cruiser parked at the curb. I made it to the head of the stairs in time to see my mother pass through my field of vision, an open magazine trailing in her hand as she went to answer the door.

"Oh, is something wrong?" She sounded surprised. I could imagine her taking a step backward, her hand rising to her mouth when she saw the officer standing at the door.

"Yes, I'm afraid there is, ma'am. Is the rector here?" A deep voice so low I had to strain to hear it, a voice I recognized at once. I knew she wouldn't like him calling her 'ma'am.' More than once I'd heard her say that the only people who used the term were the ones who think you're too old and too decrepit to look after yourself.

"No, he isn't. What is it?" Her voice sharper now, the beginning of alarm.

"It's about your son — Blake." Yes, it was definitely Mr. Hammond.

"Oh, my God." I heard something hit the floor, decided she must've dropped her magazine. "Has he been hurt?"

"No, oh no, he's not been hurt." There was a pause during which I swear he shuffled his feet on the front landing. "It's just that, well, I thought it best to let you know in person — he's down at the station."

"What's going on?" There was a sob in her voice.

"It has to do with the death of that native girl. Anna Big Sky. You've probably read about it in the papers."

"Blake wouldn't be involved — "

"I'm sorry, Mrs. Russell, but it seems he is." His voice was louder now, more sure of itself. "He came down himself." It was as if he was laying out the evidence before my mother, but then he seemed to relent, his voice softening. "He claims he wasn't involved personally, but there's others say he was. That it was his idea."

No. It would never be his idea. I started down the stairs.

"You understand," he continued, "there's no choice here — we have to keep him in custody."

My mother was crying by the time I got to her. Mr. Hammond, wearing his uniform, but looking more unsettled than I'd ever seen him — skinny and balding, his cap in his hands — had backed against the door. It was as if he needed the door to hold him upright. When he spoke again, I thought, as I often had before, that deep voice must be someone else's. It couldn't be coming from his scrawny frame.

"We knew you'd be worried when Blake . . ." He paused, swallowed, cleared his throat. "He didn't want to phone, asked if I'd come and break the news. Ashamed, I guess, but he thought you ought to know the circumstances right away."

I put my arm around my mother. "No," she said, but she was talking to him, not to me. Her shoulder quivered beneath her blouse.

Mr. Hammond stood in the doorway, looking embarrassed, his cap clasped over his crotch, as if that bit of apparel was all that kept him from being naked. His left hand suddenly abandoned the cap and began to work its way across the door, moving like something independent of the rest of him, until it finally reached the knob. "I'm sorry to have to bring you this kind of news about your son. I . . . I always liked Blake." His hand was turning the knob. "You can see him any time you want. But what you really ought to do is get yourselves a good lawyer. That's about the best advice I can give you." He had the door open now, and was edging toward it. He ducked his head toward my mother. "Sorry about . . . the bad news," he said. This was weird, but then I thought, sure, it's because my father isn't here — he was expecting to talk to my father. He glanced at me, nodded, and backed out of the house, pulling the door shut as he went. Mr. Hammond, I thought, what an awful job he's got.

My mother's shoulder was suddenly like iron beneath my hand.

"Get your father," she said. "He's over at the church."

"You going to be okay?"

"Get him now."

When I went to grab my bike, the cruiser was pulling away from the curb, its brake lights flashing once as it turned the corner.

Blake, I thought, he went down to the station just to tell them he wasn't involved. What was the good of doing that?

~·~·~

I should have been asleep when they returned from the police station, but I was still fully dressed, lying on my bed, watching the way the shadows on my ceiling moved, slowly at first, then picking up speed, darting across the room whenever a car on the street outside passed in front of our house. Once, when the shadow stopped halfway across the room, I knew they were home. Without turning on the light, I rose from my bed, pulled off my clothes, and got into my pyjamas. Let them think they woke me up.

There was conversation below, nothing I could detect as words, but a low murmur of sounds running together. I didn't even pause at the head of the stairs. I needed to know. The stairs creaked and clattered beneath my bare feet, the hum of conversation ceasing. They were in the living room, the two of them standing there, the coffee table between them. I remember noticing the globe on the coffee table, slowly spinning as if the whole world was out of control. Someone must've swiped it with a hand.

"What happened?" I asked. "What's going on?"

"You should be in bed," my mother said. She slumped down on the couch, staring not a me, but at the globe, watching it come slowly to a halt. Her eyes were red.

"Barb, he needs to know the situation." My father sat down beside her, patted her once on the knee.

"He already knows." She was staring at the globe, talking about me as if I wasn't standing just across the room.

My father patted her knee again and raised his eyes to me. "Four boys are being held in the death of Anna Big Sky. For questioning." He paused, his lips opening and closing before he continued. As if he was having trouble finding words. "Your brother's one of them." His eyes swung from me to my mother and back again. "The police think . . . Lord, help us, they think the boys murdered her." He reached for my mother's hand and took it in his own. "Blake swears he didn't touch her — he wasn't even there."

"You believe him?"

"Of course, I believe him. Why would he lie to us?"

I thought the answer was obvious, but I kept my mouth shut, kept staring at him. My father must have noticed some subtle change in my expression. "Blake went down to the station after school," he added. "Wanted to tell them what he knew. Those aren't the actions of a guilty person."

Unless he's trying to make himself look good. But I didn't say it.

My mother pulled her hand free, began to rub her upper arms as if she were cold. "It doesn't matter," she said. "They're going to charge him — just like the others."

"That's a mistake. He went to see them of his own accord. Told them everything."

"Yeah," I said, "but only after Crime Stoppers heard and — "

"Exactly," she said, and now her tone was harsh. "They already knew."

"Yes, I guess they did." My father again.

"You know they did." For the first time since I had come down the stairs my mother looked at me. "You just had to call the hot line, didn't you? Before Blake could get there. You," she paused, still staring at me, scowling now, "turned them in, named them all."

"Not Blake. I never said his name."

She rose from the couch, her eyes on me all the time, took a step toward me.

I wondered if she was going to strike me. Her eyes were wide, unfocused. She took another step. Hesitated.

"I can't deal with this," she said. "I'm going up to bed." She turned abruptly and started for the stairs.

"You go ahead," my father said. "I'm going to sit here awhile and think." He watched her go, but she gave no indication that she'd heard him speak. When she disappeared into the hall, he glanced at me. "It's late. You ought to be in bed."

"Yeah, sure. I'm gonna get a glass of milk." I walked to the fridge, pulled out the milk, opened the dish washer and retrieved a clean glass. When I finished pouring the milk, I glanced back into the living room. My father was still seated on the couch, leaning slightly forward, his head bent, hands flopped awkwardly beside him. When I set the milk back in the fridge and closed the door, his body gave a little jerk, almost as if he were suddenly aware of someone watching him. He stood up then, reached for the newspaper which was folded on the coffee table, picked it up, and sat back down on the easy chair, shifting as if trying to find a comfortable spot. I took a long swallow of milk while he opened the paper. He held it in front of him, both pages open, but as long as I stood, drinking my milk in the kitchen, he never turned a page, never moved his head. I think his mind was focused somewhere far beyond the paper.

"No, I can't leave it this way."

That's what I think she said. My mother's words came from the direction of the stairs, were barely audible, but now I heard her footsteps approaching from the hall.

She hurried into the living room where my father was seated in the easy chair, reading the paper, or pretending to read it. He gave no sign that he heard her coming. The floor lamp above him made his bald spot shine over the front page headlines. He didn't lower his paper until my mother stopped immediately in front of him. When he looked up and saw her there, he must have been troubled by what he saw, for he rose at once, took her firmly by the shoulders, "Barbara," he said, but her hands flew up, and she was reaching over his arms, one hand after the other, slapping him in the face.

"Sure, Blair made the call," she said, "but it was your fault. Advice for a friend, you said, but you knew. The whole time, didn't you? You told him what to do. He had to do what was right." That was what she said, her words angry at first, then sarcastic, and almost indistinguishable from the sobs that separated them.

My father kept his hands on her shoulders, his head swinging slightly from side to side as each blow ricocheted off his cheekbones, but he never tried to stop her. Though she was weeping now, and gasping for breath, she kept slapping his face. I wondered if I should grab her and pull her away from him, but when I took a step toward her my father shook his head. As he did, my mother struck again and, with his head twisted to one side, she caught him in the nose.

"And now — your son — your own son — he's innocent — and he's in jail — " her weeping as loud as her words " — for some girl we don't even know — an Indian." She stopped hitting him, her eyes suddenly wide with alarm. "Lord," she said, "oh, Lord!" Then she fell against him, collapsed into his arms, her wails partially smothered against his chest, but continuing, rising and falling, cries like those of an animal trying to tear its leg from a trap. My father rested his head on top of hers and held her a long time with his eyes shut. Held her until her cries were silent shudders, until her body quit shaking. I don't know how long that took. It might have been five minutes, might have been even more. At first there was a slight trickle of blood from his left nostril, but it stopped running and eventually it looked as if somehow he had spilled chocolate sauce on his upper lip. When my mother was finally quiet, he half-carried, half-walked her to the couch, where he laid her down, pulled the afghan from the back of the couch and tucked it around her. He noticed me then, still standing at the kitchen door.

"Go to bed," he said. "We need some sleep — all of us."

When I got upstairs, I stood at the window, staring down at the dark yard, the lilac bushes lost in shadow, one weak patch of light falling from our front window. I wondered what the hell my mother thought. That I was out to get my brother? Was that it? Did she really think I'd put them through all this suffering just to nail him? To frame my own brother? She didn't know a thing — neither one of them did. They figured he was innocent.

Later, quite some time after I had slid into bed, I heard my door open. Footsteps cautiously approached the bed.

"Blair, you awake?" My father whispering in case by some chance I was asleep already.

I rolled toward the sound. "Uh-huh."

"I'm sorry you had to be downstairs for that." His voice was still only a whisper. "You have to understand, your mother was very wrought up. She's not herself tonight. If she were, you know as well as I do, she would never have said what she said — there at the end."

"I know that."

He did something then he hadn't done in years, leaned over the bed and kissed me lightly on the forehead, his lips like dry parchment on my skin. "Good night, son," he said, and left the room.

Neither then, nor afterwards did it strike me as odd that what had worried him so much it brought him to my room, what he didn't want me to misinterpret in any way was her dismissal of Anna as an Indian, and not the blows she'd rained upon his cheeks.

～～～

When we circled the coaches after warming up for Saturday's big game against Diefenbaker High, we all shoved toward the centre of the circle, slapped our right hands together, shouted in unison, "We can win, yes we can, we're together, every man," but I don't think any of us believed it. We all knew that four of our first stringers were sitting downtown in jail. Three of them were irreplaceable. Yeah, and this game was for the league championship; with the southern final next week and the provincial final the week after that, they wouldn't even consider postponing this one.

I hadn't felt much like dressing for the game — football didn't seem important anymore — but then I thought that, since my brother had screwed up, and let his teammates down too, there should be at least one Russell on the team. But it wasn't letting his teammates down that got to me. I was furious because of what he'd done to Anna — helped to do. Still, I knew he'd never have been involved if it weren't for that damned Jordan Phelps. That, at least, was what I needed to believe.

Besides, I was going to play. Morris Ackerman had been moved from defence to offence, given the impossible task of replacing Phelps at wide receiver, and I was going to take Morris's spot in the defensive backfield. For the whole game. That shouldn't have mattered, of course — playing football was nothing compared to a dead girl — but to tell the truth I was kind of excited to be starting on defence instead of standing on the sidelines like some jerk-off who couldn't play.

Diefenbaker won the toss and chose to receive. For the first time ever, I was on the field for the kickoff, my legs shaking so hard I was surprised they held me up. Then the ball was in the air and I was running downfield, keeping in my lane, a blocker hitting me, his shoulder hard in my chest, and it was okay — I wasn't nervous anymore. Except he hit me again, and again. When someone finally brought the runner down at mid-field, I was still trying to shake off the blocker and nowhere near the play.

Diefenbaker had a running game, but they threw the ball often enough that you knew you couldn't count on a run. My problem was that I had to cover the slotback until I was sure they weren't going to pass to him, then come up fast and try to stop the runner who was going full speed by then with at least one blocker out in front. I was dodging blockers, slapping at them, shoving them, grabbing their arms, fighting to get through them and lay my hands on the runner. Once I faked to the left, lunged right, and made a blocker miss me, but I was off balance, almost staggering as I went for the runner, and he put his head down and drove me backwards, carrying me half a dozen yards before I got him stopped. I remember Ivan Buchko slapped me on the butt and said, "Way to go, Blair. You're getting it."

We finally stopped them on our fourteen yard line, one of our linemen recovering a fumble. Now it was our turn.

Our first play was a run, off-tackle, for a mere three yards. Then Mac Kelsey, our second string quarterback threw a pass, but he hurried it, throwing before the receiver turned around, bouncing if off his shoulder, and we had to kick.

It seemed as if I was back on the field before I caught my breath. Yeah, Blake, I thought, if you weren't so stupid, you'd be here yourself, and we'd have a quarterback who knew how to complete a pass. And then for some reason I felt crummy, as if

I was crazy to be out here playing football in the snow, but no matter how I felt I wasn't going to quit.

For a while, it almost seemed as if the Diefenbaker team had made a deal with the ref that allowed them extra players on the field. Every time I tried to stop a run, another blocker hammered me. I swear, there were blockers everywhere. In fact, I made two tackles on the far side of the field, but only one on my own side, because when the play went to the far side the blockers were hitting someone else. Of course, by the time I tackled the runner over there he'd gained at least a dozen yards. Football was too much like the rest of life, things not working out the way you want them to.

It was a long afternoon.

And a lopsided score. In the end, a team that in normal circumstances we might have beaten, outscored us 20 to 7. When the final whistle blew, I was battered and breathless — and the happiest I'd been in days. There was something satisfying about being out there all the time, being a part of it all, those seconds of tension before the ball was snapped, then the sudden release, breaking into action, running, shifting direction, muscles straining, hurling my body at someone else. Once, in the fourth quarter, they threw a short pass to the slotback I was covering. He ran right at me, faked to the outside, then cut inside, running parallel to the line of scrimmage, looking for the ball that he knew would be coming at him. But I was right behind him, already seeing it happen. When the ball touched his fingertips, I nailed him from behind, low, my shoulder beneath his butt, my legs driving hard, and he was going over backwards, his shoulders slamming into the ground, bouncing, the ball coming loose, dribbling away. Incomplete.

Oh Blake, I thought, never have you hit a guy like that. And then I felt crummy again.

The locker room was more quiet than usual after the game, players slumped on the benches like sacks of dirty jerseys, nobody saying a thing. Yeah, and it wasn't just the loss that we were thinking of, with Anna dead and four of our teammates in jail. When Coach Ramsey came in, he stomped through the room, kicked a locker and slammed himself onto the bench without a word. I felt the bench shudder beneath me. Coach Conley was right behind him. He walked a little circle in front of us, his eyes resting an instant on each of us before he spoke.

"Well, guys," he said, "it was a tough way to end the season. But it was a good season, and I don't want you to forget that. You won every game but this one, and this afternoon you had a lot going against you." He paused and looked around the room again, maybe wondering if he should get specific or simply leave it unsaid. "To tell you the truth, I think I'm more proud of you right now than I've been all year. You all knew you were up against it today, but you never quit trying. Maybe the score was a little one-sided, but I'll tell you something: right now, that other team is every bit as tired and bruised as you are. They had a tough game, and they know it. Sure, they had more talent today, but you guys kept going at them all afternoon. You hit them, and you hit them, and then you got up and hit them again. I just want you to know I feel like it's an honour to be your coach."

I can't say that anyone around the room was smiling or looking proud, but at least nobody resembled a sack of laundry anymore.

"Well, it's been a long afternoon," said the coach. "Right now, you all look as if you could use a nice hot shower. Go ahead, guys, and don't worry about your lockers. You can clean them out Monday after school." He grinned at us, or tried to grin perhaps, then stepped into his office, and I thought how calm he seemed. We'd just lost the biggest game of the year, and already he had it in perspective.

Most of the players looked as if they'd come back to life. They started hauling their jerseys off, getting out of their equipment, bits of conversation starting up here and there throughout the room, some of the guys drifting off to the shower room. Coach Ramsey was still sitting on the bench. When the guy between us headed for the showers, Ramsey slid toward me. "You little shit," he said, his voice surprisingly quiet. "Don't think I didn't see you going at your brother the other day at practice. The day he took off. When I ask him what's going on, you know what he says? He says, 'My stupid brother told.' I didn't know what he meant. Not then."

Ramsey wasn't even looking at me, and I didn't respond. He rose suddenly and stepped in front of me.

"Right away he's in jail — him and the other three. And who turned them in? Not too hard to figure out, is it? Wasn't for you, they'd of been out there where they should of been. Playing."

Damned if I was going to give him the satisfaction of knowing he was getting to me. I kept gazing straight ahead, my eyes focused on his midriff, where his Lightning jacket was pushed out by the roll of flab that hung over his belt.

"You listening to me? If there was even half a brain in that ugly head of yours, we'd of had all our best players going today. That Diefenbaker bunch wouldn't of touched us."

I knew he wanted to shake me, but I never raised my eyes. A gold button wavered in front of me, some of the paint peeled away, a dull brass beneath it. The cloth was pulled tight around the button.

"Half a brain and you would of waited till the game was over before you did something stupid."

I wondered if he could see me shiver. Any minute now, and he was going to slug me. Yeah, if I didn't hit him first.

"They all could of played—every one of them. You get what I'm saying, shithead? All you had to do was wait."

I was leaning back as far as I could without falling off the bench, but he was pressing toward me, his bulky stomach so close the button almost touched my nose.

"I'm talking to you, you little bugger!"

The button shifted, jumped suddenly.

"Whoa! Enough of this."

Coach Conley had Ramsey by the shoulder, hauled him around, jerked him almost off his feet. Coach Conley was yelling at him, and suddenly I thought, that's funny, he never yells at us. "Leave it alone. Just leave it alone."

"Yeah, but — "

"Shut the hell up. Right now."

The two of them jaw to jaw in the middle of the room, my teammates backing away from them as if someone had lit a fuse there in the locker room, and they didn't want to be caught in the blast. All you could hear was breathing, harsh and quick, from the two men, I guess, and maybe from the players watching them. Then Coach Conley stepped away from Ramsey and nodded toward his office. "Maybe, we should go in there and have a chat," he said to Ramsey, his voice as composed as it was in health class.

When Ramsey wheeled around, he gave me a dirty look and said, "The least you could of done was sit tight. One bloody week — that was all we needed."

Coach Conley didn't wait for him to leave the room before he came to me. "Don't concern yourself about this," he said, laying his hand on my shoulder. "Nothing here was your fault. Coach Ramsey likes to win — puts a lot of work into winning, you understand. Sometimes he loses track of other things." He was looking down at me, his grey eyes mild as a summer shower. He glanced at the other players, paused. I guess he wanted to say something reassuring for all of us.

"Eight years ago," he said, "we had a terrific running game. Tank Tinsley was our fullback, big and fast too, best runner I ever coached. Kid could run through a locked door. We went to the provincial final that year, up in North Battleford. Would have won it too, but the night before the game Tank decided the curfew didn't apply to him. Oh no, he had to try the hotel bar and see if maybe in a strange town he could pull some beer. Head coach back then was Coach Grenier. He'd told everybody on the team exactly what I told the bunch of you — that anybody breaking curfew was going to get himself benched. He benched Tinsley and we lost. If Mr. Ramsey had been coaching with us then, I don't suppose he would've approved, but I have to say I admired Coach Grenier. The man had guts." He looked around the room again. "You do what you have to do — that's the way it is. The way it has to be."

His hand was on my shoulder all the time he spoke. When he finished, he gave my shoulder a squeeze and started to follow Ramsey into his office, but he stopped and turned back to us.

"Pulling beer is one thing," he said, "but it doesn't get anybody killed. I don't know what's going on with those four boys, but the police figure they know something, and you can bet it's serious. You guys best hit the showers and get on home."

No one moved until he'd disappeared into his office and the door was closed. Then everyone began to talk.

I thought they might want to kill me, but they just wanted to know, was I the one who turned them in.

"Not my brother, no," I told them, "but the other guys — they're guilty as hell."

When Morris Ackerman said Coach Ramsey was right, I should've had brains enough to wait, Ivan Buchko told him to shut his face, there were more important things than winning.

~~~

That night at supper we had TV dinners, thin slices of turkey, mushy potatoes, mixed vegetables, a gob of cherry pudding, all in separate compartments on what looked like cardboard plates — my mother said she wasn't much interested in cooking. Nor in the game either when my father brought it up. What she was interested in, what she wanted to talk about was the lawyer. How could they be sure Wanda McKinnel was the right one to hire? Had they perhaps made a mistake not getting a man? No, my father said, she's got a good reputation. Yes, but in these circumstances —

"Jim Hammond swears by her," my father said. "Besides, I liked her when I talked to her. She made sense." He turned to me. "Which reminds me, we need to have a little talk."

"Now?"

"When supper's done."

It was suddenly like eating leather, but I got it all down, and when I was finished, he led me up to the den, waved me toward the chair beside his desk, and closed the door. He sat down and leaned across the desk toward me.

"Listen now: there's something I need to get absolutely straight. That night you came wanting advice for your friend, you weren't asking for a friend, were you?"

"I guess not."

"Your mom and I weren't jumping to conclusions?"

I shook my head.

He studied me a minute, his eyes not blinking once. "It was Blake you were worried about."

"Uh-huh."

"Why in the world would you think Blake would be involved in . . . in the death of Anna Big Sky?" He had hesitated, but he finished in a rush. When I didn't answer, he continued, "Why did you think Blake was guilty?"

I couldn't tell him what they'd done to Amber — what he'd done. "It wasn't just him," I said. "It was Jordan Phelps and — "

"But you think Blake is guilty."

"I guess so — yeah."

He shook his head. "You have any reason for thinking this way?" I could tell he was trying to keep his voice down.

"Sure."

"Come on. Out with it."

I had to tell him something, and when I started it came gushing out. "He's just like the rest of them — doing whatever Jordan Phelps wants. And Jordan hated Anna — because she showed him up for the loser he is. I saw it happen — in the hall at school — and, man, he wanted to get her back. And Blake was mad at her because he took her out once and she didn't want to go out again, but he said he knew he could get her to go with him, and he must've talked it over with Jordan and the other guys, and they got her out there in the country, and that's where they did it."

My father shook his head again. "That's your evidence?"

I nodded.

"You're wrong, you know? You need to talk to him. Wanda McKinnel says she's almost positive Blake had nothing to do with that girl's death. She thinks he was concerned about the other boys, trying to get them to do what was right, turn themselves in."

"She doesn't know him like I do."

"Know him? I don't think you know a bloody thing." He was half out of his chair, his voice loud and angry, but he got his hands on the desk and pushed himself back into his chair. I felt sorry for him then. He wanted to make everything right for Blake, and he couldn't do a thing. "What is it with you? You want your brother in jail?"

"No. Of course not." But I was the one who'd phoned Crime Stoppers.

"Get out of here, will you? I need to think."

I had fled to my room, but it was too quiet up there, the walls closing in around me, like it was me in a cell instead of Blake, and I'd come back down stairs. I thought about phoning Evan to come over, but he'd probably want to know what was going on with Blake, and I didn't want to talk about it. I had the living room all to myself and turned on the television. My mother was in the bedroom, staying out of sight, I guess, that was about all that she was up to, that and crying; my father was still in the den, by now probably working on the next day's sermon. It had to be done. Must have been hard for him to write a sermon when he was worried about Blake in jail and mad at me to boot. Still, if you didn't know any better, you might think it wasn't much different from any other Saturday night. At our house, Saturday nights were never a lively time. Usually, I'd be out somewhere with Evan, but if I was home I'd often hear my father going over his sermon, practising it out loud, working on his emphases and pauses, adding examples that he hoped would get through even to the people in the back pew. He liked to say that the ideas came from the Lord, but it was his job to keep the congregation from drifting off to sleep.

I lay down on the couch, hoping I could concentrate on the hockey game. The Leafs were leading Boston three to two, players slamming one another into the boards, ice chips flying, the glass shaking, and I thought, maybe I can do this, think about the game and nothing else, the puck dumped ahead, everybody chasing it, but my eyes were heavy and I kept sliding off, missing portions of the action. Time and time again a new line would be breaking in on goal, and I hadn't seen them leave the bench. Then the score was tied, and I had missed the goal. Once the Leaf winger swooped behind the net, blond hair flying below his helmet, the puck on his stick as he cut around a player, one foot striking the back of the goal, catching, and he was off balance, already falling when the Bruin defenceman smashed him against the boards. His head struck the boards, snapped back, and he fell to the ice. Lay there without any sign of motion. Even the announcer was silent for a few seconds. Someone from the bench was bent over him, the trainer, I guess, examining his head. He seemed to be unconscious. When the trainer pulled his helmet off, his hair wasn't blond anymore, but dark and curly, a gash across his cheekbone, his eyelids beginning to flutter, and when those eyes finally opened, my brother was looking up at me.

I sat up so fast my feet slammed onto the floor.

The trainer was bent over him once more, shielding him from view. Seemed to be whispering in his ear. Then he was moving one hand, the other hand, both his legs, and I was breathing again. Two players got his arms over their shoulders, lifted him. His legs splayed and dragging, they skated him toward the bench, the crowd applauding, and it was the Leaf winger they were clapping for, blond hair falling on his shoulders, not my brother after all.

I grabbed the remote and turned off the game. Sat hunched forward on the couch, staring at the empty screen, trying not to think, but my brother was in jail, and I had helped put him there.

No, that wasn't right. He was the one who knew Anna would go out with him, who'd driven to the old McAuley place, taken her there — I knew it as sure as if I'd been there myself to see him — and then everything had gone wrong and she was dead. They'd killed her, God, she was gone forever. He must have been crazy, yeah, drunk and crazy, but that was no excuse. He made his own choices.

Sure, I chickened out at the last second, couldn't say his name, but he was just as guilty as the other guys. The buggers.

Was there any chance that I was wrong? No, the police were holding him — just like the rest of them — the police wouldn't have it wrong.

I was so damned tired — too tired to think straight. I needed to get some sleep, but I wasn't sure I had the strength to make it up the stairs to bed. I dug my fists into my eyes, tried to rub the sleep away, but my knuckles were wet when I looked down at them.

Some time later, I realized I was lying on the couch again. The light on the end table by the easy chair was still on, the one we always used while watching T.V., but the room seemed darker. Someone had turned the hall light off, yes, and pulled the afghan over me. I checked my watch. Twelve-thirty. I swung my legs onto the floor, the muscles stiff and aching, but I knew I could make it up to bed.

When I reached the top of the stairs, I saw that the light was off in the den, but passing the door, I felt my heart surge, my breath halt an instant, then come back in a rush. On the other side of the dark room, just visible in the pale light from the window, my father sat at his desk, his head bent, his shoulders slouched forward. He had to be lost in thought, his mind far away and troubled, or he would have heard me on the stairs, maybe even heard me gasp. When I noticed his hands clasped together before him, I knew that he was praying. For what seemed like many minutes, I remained at the door, standing awkwardly, half-turned toward the den, watching him, but he never shifted his position, and at last, when I felt one calf begin to cramp, I tiptoed off to bed.

NINE

Though the blind was drawn, sunshine bled all around it and filled the room with dusky light. The house beyond my room was absolutely quiet, no sound of traffic from the street outside. My parents must have slept in. But no, of course, they wouldn't do that. Not on a Sunday morning. They'd left me in bed, decided, maybe, that I needed sleep as much as church, and gone quietly off together. Yeah, and I wondered what they'd say afterwards, when someone down for coffee asked them where the boys were this morning. "Blair's sacked out at home, and Blake's sawing logs down in the city jail." Not bloody likely.

Yes, but what could they say?

What must it be like for them, I wondered, with one son implicated in a killing and another who'd turned him in? Everybody in the congregation would have read the articles about the killing, seen the television news, the stubble field with its crust of snow, wind stirring, fresh snow beginning to drift over the fluorescent paint. They'd all know who Anna Big Sky was, but no other names had been released, of course, because at seventeen my brother and his friends were underage. Still, Palliser was a small city. Someone would know, and there'd be talk. The guys on the team would tell their friends. Eventually the names would get around. Eventually — hell, a lot of kids at school knew already. Some of their parents would too, and they'd be phoning each other.

I hoped none of them had phoned my father yet.

How was he going to stand up in the chancel and get through a sermon in front of them? How could my mother sit in the choir and raise her voice in praise as if this were just another Sunday? Would her voice crack on "The Lord's Prayer," or would it rise above all the others as they sang, "And forgive us our trespasses"? And what about my father, leading everyone in prayer, his deep intonations audible even as the voices of the congregation mixed with his? "To you all hearts are open, all desires known, and from you no secrets are hidden." For years on Sunday mornings I'd repeated the words along with everybody else, getting through them by rote, barely listening, but today they meant something new.

And what would it be like for my parents afterwards, leaving the empty church and coming home to the rectory when one of their sons was missing?

It was almost eleven-thirty. With any kind of crowd going up to take communion, the service would last at least another twenty minutes, and then people would wander downstairs for coffee, taking their time, some of them standing at the front to chat, others clustered in groups around the small tables, sipping their coffees, munching on cookies, Mrs. Sandeman getting up half a dozen times, strolling casually to the front as if no one would notice her grabbing another cookie. I had lots of time.

Out of bed, into my jeans and t-shirt, downstairs to the kitchen.

I pulled the Edwards can from the freezer where my mother stored it to keep the coffee fresh. Measured out enough for four cups, filled the perc with water to the proper level, plugged it in and got it going. Then back to the freezer for the bagels, three of them. Tried to slice one in half, but it was like sawing wood with a breadknife. I put them in the microwave to thaw. Fifty seconds on high, and they were so hot I had to juggle them getting them back to the cutting board, but I could cut them now, slicing them like bread. It felt good to be doing something. Then a coating of tomato sauce, slices of cheese spread on the sauce, some pieces of Ready Crisp Bacon on top of the cheese. Laid the six halves on a pan. Cranked up the oven, left its door cocked open and ready, set the dishes on the table. As soon as I heard footsteps on the porch, I'd slide the pan into the oven.

"That was good," my father said when we had finished eating, but his voice was lifeless. During the meal, they'd mainly talked about Mrs. Elmitt, how worked up she was at church, telling everyone about her husband's heart attack, getting more worked up with every telling. My father didn't usually visit at the hospital on Sunday afternoons, but he thought today he'd better go.

"Nice to come home," said my mother when she had swallowed her last bite of bagel, "and have the meal ready for the table." She swept her serviette across her lower lip, wiped away a daub of sauce.

"It's a bloody shame," my father added, "that Blake couldn't be here to share it with us."

"Yes," said my mother, a catch in her voice, "yes, it is." Now her serviette was rubbing at her eyes.

There was no sound in the room except for the scritch, scritch of paper grazing skin.

"We can't go on like this, you know," my father said. He glared across the table at me. "Your brother's sitting in that bloody jail, all kinds of accusations levelled at him. He's worried out of his head, and we're bellied up to the table, going on about how good your pizza-bagels are." His eyes were red, but they looked as if they had sunk an inch into his head. "You need to get down there and see him. He wants to talk to you."

~~~

I went into the police station with Wanda McKinnel. I was nervous about seeing my brother, didn't know what I'd say.

Mr. Hammond and my father were certain we had the right lawyer to handle my brother's case. Ms. McKinnel was what my father called her. I don't know if that meant she wasn't married or she didn't want people to know her marital status. She was a reader, Mr. Hammond said, in a book club with his wife. Generous too. Every summer she sponsored a writer at the local authors' festival.

I wondered if Ms. McKinnel would take me down to the cells, wondered if they'd be bare cement and bars, shadows and darkness, a single light bulb hanging in a hall between the cells, but as soon as she finished talking to the officer in charge she led me into a medium-sized room and motioned to a chair. She said she'd met with Blake before, "a cursory meeting" was how she put it. There were other chairs and a table in the middle of the room, three filing cabinets against one wall. I looked around for one-way glass like on TV, but all I saw was a pane of frosted glass on the door. The outer wall had three large windows, but they weren't even barred. A narrow band of wallpaper ran around the room just below the windows, hunting scenes with Irish setters on it. Irish setters, for Pete's sake. There was a large SGI calendar above the filing cabinets and on the other wall, above a metal radiator, a pale rectangle where a picture must have hung at some time in the past. Had a prisoner grabbed it off the wall and used it as a weapon, smashed someone over the head with it, maybe even cut his wrists with broken glass? No, I was being silly; this was just an ordinary meeting room, probably the very place where the mayor sat down for long and boring discussions with members of the police commission. Still, except for that calendar, there were no pictures anywhere. It had to make me wonder.

When my brother came into the room, the first things I saw were the handcuffs, his wrists bound in front of him. An officer pushed the door closed behind him. Blake was wearing a sweat shirt and blue jeans, exactly what he'd wear at home, but his jeans were hanging low at the waist. He was walking awkwardly, shambling along, and for an instant I thought he must be wearing leg-irons, but when I looked at his feet, I saw his shoes flopping on his feet, their laces removed. Then I noticed that his belt was gone. I still didn't catch on for a while, but when I did, I got a queasy feeling.

Blake circled the table and sat down in a chair across from us, immediately shoved his hands beneath the table, pushing the cuffs out of sight. Never once looked at me.

"Something awful's going on," he said to Ms. McKinnel. "The other guys — I can hear them in their cells — they're all saying I'm a rat. They won't even talk to me." His eyes flicked in my direction, but returned at once to her. "They're trying to put all the blame on me." His words were low and rushed. "Not for turning them in. For killing Anna." He paused, took a deep breath. "What's going to happen to me?"

"If you're not involved," said Ms. McKinnel, "I'd say there's a good chance everything's going to work out just fine. It may take a while, that's all." She sounded confident, I thought, and also somewhat pompous. "I had a talk with the police chief after your father came to see me. I'm afraid you're right about one thing. The other boys are trying to lay the blame on you, but you mustn't worry. The police have seized the Foster car." She paused, staring at him, as if searching for some kind of reaction. "The chief said he's got some doubts about their story. Nothing he's heard so far has him convinced."

Blake leaned forward, his lower lip trembling as he spoke. "What are they saying?"

"The Foster boy claims he had a date with Anna Big — "

"That could be true. I saw the two of them together — driving in his father's car." Blake was nodding his head. "Toyota," he added, "a silver Camry."

"You may be right," said Ms. McKinnel. She studied him a moment, gazing steadily into his eyes, looking, I suppose, for some sign of guilt. "Young Foster claims you drove up behind them."

"No way!"

Ms. McKinnel held up her hand to silence him, continued speaking. "They were necking, and suddenly their car was blocked in — you flung the door open, dragged him out, started beating her."

Blake was shaking his head all the while she spoke, nervously, I thought, hopelessly, but then his expression changed, becoming merely thoughtful. "The bastards," he said, "that must be how it was."

Ms. McKinnel looked as puzzled as I felt. "You mean they're telling the truth."

"Of course not." He seemed disgusted. "You think I could beat up Vaughn Foster? He's all muscles."

"He said he was too drunk to stop you. You hauled him out of the car, hit him in the stomach and he started to vomit — that's all he remembers. He says he must've passed out."

"The lying bastard!" He glanced down at the table. "Sorry, but this is really getting to me."

"None of it's true?"

"I wasn't there." He sat back in his chair, and turned to me, gazed right at me for the first time since he'd come into the room. "You know I could never handle Foster."

I shrugged.

"Jesus Christ, you want me in jail?" He turned at once to Ms. McKinnel. "Pardon my tongue," he said, "but my brother — " he glared at me " — I don't know what's with you anymore."

"That's right. Your father wanted the two of you to talk." She looked from him to me, and back again. Stood up abruptly. "Perhaps, a few minutes alone together would be useful. I'll be just down the hall."

Neither of us moved until the door had clicked shut behind her. I was watching the closed door when Blake spoke. "You still think I had something to do with it, that I helped kill her. That's what's going on, isn't it?"

I shrugged again.

"You shrug like that one more time, I'm gonna rip your head off." He paused, waited at least twenty seconds, leaned toward me. "I asked you a question."

"I . . . don't know . . . what to think."

"You really think I could do something like that?"

"Maybe . . . I don't know. I saw you piss on — "

"Okay, I lied, yeah, I did that. But I was drunk, I didn't know her, she was just — "

"Amber, she was Amber Saunders. She didn't deserve that kind of — "

"You think I don't know that?" He'd been leaning toward me, his eyes full of anger, but now he slumped backward, seemed to cringe into his chair. His eyes filled with tears. "Oh, Lord, I'm so ashamed of that. It's why I lied to you. Seems like weeks now, I haven't been able to look you in the face. Knowing that you knew. That you might tell Mom and Dad. Hell, I've hardly looked anybody in the face."

I was furious with him. "I'd never tell them that." It was true, I realized, and suddenly I knew why. "My God, it would destroy them. I wouldn't believe you could do such a thing. Except I saw you do it."

His words were barely audible. "And I am so sorry." His eyes were wet with tears, and mine must have been wet too. He was a blur across the table. Still, I could see that he had more to say. His voice was firmer when he spoke again. "You wouldn't tell Mom and Dad, but you told the police."

He wasn't being fair.

"Not about Amber. About Anna. She was dead, and someone had to pay. I saw where she fell; I saw the piss in the snow."

My brother flinched. But then he reached toward me, both hands flying up from underneath the table. The cuff on one hand clanked against the table top as he grabbed my hand, and I suddenly felt sick inside. "I liked Anna!" he said. "I wouldn't — I'd never do a thing like that again. No matter how drunk I was." He held my hand so tight I thought he might break it. "And I wasn't drunk. The whole night I never had a single beer." He saw that he hadn't swayed me yet, he'd have to put it into words. "I'd never piss on Anna. You can't believe I'm that kind of scum."

There was so much intensity in his eyes, so much heat it felt as if the air between us might ignite.

"Come on," I said at last. "I never called you scum." It wasn't much, but it was all that I could give him then. After what must have been another minute, both of us glaring at the other, my mouth clenched shut, he released my hand. Although it stung like mad, I wasn't going to rub it.

"Ever since . . . since that football party, you've been looking at me like I was just a piece of shit." There was an eraser on the table in front of him. He placed one hand upon it and began to rub it back and forth beneath his palm. "A dirty piece of dog shit you'd stepped on by accident. Which is exactly how I felt."

"I never thought that way."

"Oh yeah? And something else you've got to understand. I wasn't there. You need to get that through your thick head."

"I never said you were."

"What?"

"When I phoned Crime Stoppers. I just couldn't do it. The others, sure — but not you."

Blake reached for me again, but I pulled my hand away just in time. "You stupid ass," he said, "that's why they're after me. No bloody wonder. They think I ratted on them."

"But you went down to the police station — "

"Yeah, because I thought you turned me in. I had to clear my name. And now — thanks to you — I'm done for."

I was about to tell him, sorry, no, that's not how it was meant to be, but I heard the door open, footsteps entering the room.

"I hope you two ironed a few things out," Ms. McKinnel said. She took her seat again, set her briefcase on the table, opened it, and pulled out a pad of foolscap. "We've got some serious work to do here. I need to be sure I've got everything absolutely right about what happened that night. Where you were and when. Everything you saw." She'd been gazing across the table at my brother, but now she turned to me. "I think it would be best, Blair, if you'd leave us to it."

When I left the room, my brother still sat with his head down, the eraser sliding back and forth beneath his fingers, the light from overhead glinting on the handcuffs.

~·~·~

"You work things out with Blake?" my father asked.

I started to shrug but caught myself. "We had a talk, yeah." Didn't we though? And now I knew I should have given the cops his name too, but oh no, I had to spare him, and now the other guys thought he was the one who turned them in. Oh man, what a screw-up.

"I don't know what's come between you," he said. "Put the two of you in one room, you can hardly breathe the air it's so thick with tension."

"I guess . . . we haven't . . . been getting along all that well." My comment was as limp as it sounded.

"You don't know how it tears up your mother — the two of you . . . and now . . . everything else that's happened."

He couldn't say it. I think he was feeling it even more than my mother. Did he believe that Blake was guilty — no matter what he claimed — was that what was going on?

"You still think he's guilty?" The words seemed wrenched from deep within him. "That's got to be what it is. You really think he had something to do with that girl's death." When he finally looked at me, his eyes, which so often of late appeared red and tired, were pale as a mirage. I suddenly wished I could hug him.

"Yeah, I guess I did."

He took three breaths before he spoke. I could hear the inhalations.

"You did, but not now?"

"I . . . don't know."

Another three inhalations. It was weird, but his breath came out so softly that I never heard him exhale. It was as if he was only breathing in, sucking all the air from the room, sucking it in until finally he'd swell up and explode.

"Why," he asked, "why would you think he was guilty?"

If I told him what I'd seen that night in Fosters' yard, it would be like ripping out his heart. I shook my head.

"Your mother figured right away it was you who turned him in. But you already know that."

I knew it, sure, but still I felt a tremor in my stomach. I kept my mouth shut.

"Come on, Blair. Don't treat me like a fool. You're the one who came to me with that cock-and-bull story about advice for your friend at school. Wanting to know the right thing to do." When he paused, I had to look away. "Why?"

"He was acting different. Something bad had happened, I knew that, something that really bothered him, and he was always with those other guys. Everybody knew what they were like." It was crazy, I know, it didn't make any sense, but I couldn't tell my parents he'd pissed on Amber even though I'd as good as told them he'd helped kill Anna.

"Your brother swears he's done nothing wrong, but you can't seem to credit that possibility. Because something's come between you." He slowly shook his head. "Do not judge," he said, "so that you may not be judged."

"What's that supposed to mean?"

"Why do you see the speck in your neighbour's eye, but do not notice the log in your own eye?"

"That's the Bible, eh?"

"It is indeed. From the Gospel According to Matthew. You might want to think about it. I suspect it has some application to the present situation with you and your brother." He smiled at me, or tried to smile, hoping maybe that it would be a help to me in some strange way. He stood up.

I suppose I could be thankful he'd never mentioned Cain and Abel.

As he passed me now on his way toward the door, he dropped his hand to my shoulder, let it linger there a few seconds.

~·~·~

Night time. Pale clouds and a dim moon. The car turns from the road into an open field, its headlights off, follows a trail, stubble and snow everywhere, the stubble like a brush-cut on the head of a man going bald. Traveling too fast on the rough trail, the car bounces once, swerves, almost slides into the field, but the driver cranks the wheel, tires spinning, snow spraying behind, gets it going straight. Drives it through the narrow opening between caragana hedges, their overgrown branches reaching out as if to block the trail. The car bounces again as it hits a shallow snow-filled ditch, begins to sink, the ditch collapsing, growing, snow sucked into the crevice, its sides caving-in, but the driver guns the car, the back wheels catching something solid, and the car lurches over the edge of the crevice, back onto the trail. Slowing down, it continues another thirty yards, brake lights flashing as it rolls to a stop behind another car, a silver Camry. No door opens. The Camry's headlights are extinguished too, but its motor runs, the car a silver shadow on the snow. Voices can be heard from inside. Urgent voices. Twice the taillights flash when a wandering foot strikes the brake. Then quiet, the second car hunched down like an animal waiting to attack. Caraganas behind it, on the other three sides brush, a tangle of black trees, broken limbs, grasses soughing in the wind. High in the trees, a branch is moving too, dropping half a foot, quivering as a huge, dark hawk lands, its eyes glowing red, brighter than Mars.

A door opens on the second car, no sign of an interior light, a leg swung over the frame, one foot descending to the snow, another leg appears, a dark figure rising beside the car. He walks toward the trees. Toward the biggest, thickest tree where a branch sways beneath the heavy bird — it's not a hawk now, but something else — its neck stretched down and naked now, red coals gleaming in its eyes. The figure doesn't see the bird. He stops, slowly turns his head in a half-circle, nods, begins to walk again. A framework lighter than the trees around it, planks nailed together, like the skeleton of a building, a ladder beside it which the figure climbs, mounting steadily toward the swaying rope until he stands beneath it — I recognize him then — the noose falling over his head, and I look away just in time.

I sat up in bed. A gallows — but that was crazy, they didn't hang killers in Canada, not anymore, they didn't. I switched on the light. Breath still shaking in my throat, but here there was no hawk — no vulture either — and my brother, I knew, would never face a noose.

Did he do it? Help the others kill her?

I didn't think so. Had I changed my mind, or was it that I didn't want to think so?

No, there were reasons rushing in — now that it was too late — reasons I should have thought about before, but had somehow pushed aside, overlooked. Was I jealous of

Blake — was that what it was? — so mad at him I could hardly think?

For many days he'd worn his shame like that woman with the scarlet letter we'd heard about at school. She'd been knocked up — bore a child out of wedlock, was what the teacher said — and I had thought, yeah, but it took a guy to help her. And what about Blake, was he the kind of guy who'd beat up a drunk so he could screw his girl? Would he think she was just an Indian, it didn't matter what you did with one of them, would anybody ever give a damn?

He'd looked down on one girl, unconscious, shivering on the ground. Could he help to kill another?

But he liked Anna Big Sky, and I didn't think he was a racist. Sometimes he said some stupid things, sure, but I remembered the first week of school, Anna passing in the hall — before I even knew her name — some skinny guy saying, "Snooty Indian broad," and my brother telling him to stop being such a dork.

If he wasn't a racist, was it possible that he just hated women? Half the guys in school gave girls a rough time, shooting off their mouths and all, but I didn't think Blake was one of them. He'd had a steady girl when he was in grade eleven, Kathy Trimble — she always teased me when he brought her home — but they'd broken up in the summer holidays. Sure, but they were still friends. At the Freshie Dance he'd danced with her two or three times, and I sometimes saw them hanging out together in the halls. Yeah, but what about Amber Saunders? Could anything be worse than what he'd done to her? Lord, the way she must have felt when she figured out what had happened — humiliating. But he'd said he'd never do a thing like that a second time, and I knew he felt humiliated too.

I was staring at the foot of the bed, sheet and blankets in a turmoil, but there were no answers there. I lay down again.

The clock radio beside my bed, its numbers red as vulture eyes.

I needed to talk to my brother again. There was so much we had to straighten out.

TEN

The wall behind her desk was all bookcase, thick oak shelves filled from floor to ceiling with rows of books, many of them bound in leather, and magazines, law journals I suppose they were, stacks of them piled on top of books, but I kept looking at the aquarium on the middle shelf. A mermaid sat on a rock, untarnished and fragile, her skin so white you knew she'd never seen the sun, bubbles rising from her mouth, disappearing in the green plants that floated above her head. Gliding slowly around her were tropical fish, half a dozen of them, their fins barely moving. Some of them looked like miniature sharks, waiting to attack.

My parents had picked me up from school that morning, pulled me out of class after the first period. As soon as the three of us sat down on the cushioned chairs before her desk, Ms. McKinnel said her piece.

"The reason I called you in," she said, "is that Blake asked me to talk to you — so you'll understand the situation before this afternoon's hearing. I know you'll want to be in court, but we think this will make it easier."

My father nodded his head but didn't speak.

"Can we take him home after that?" my mother asked. She sat with her hands hugging her shoulders as if she were cold.

"That will depend on whether the other boys decide to change their story."

"What *is* their story?" My mother again, her fingers rubbing at her shoulders.

"They say that Blake drove up behind Vaughn Foster's car and boxed him in, that he's the one who beat the Big Sky girl."

"That's hogwash," said my father. "I don't believe it for a minute. He liked Anna Big Sky. Why would he beat her up?" He was asking Ms. McKinnel, but then he looked at me as if seeking confirmation.

Blake had said something odd when Ms. McKinnel and I had seen him at the police station, when she had told him Foster's story about how he'd blocked their car in. "The bastards, that must be how it was."

If Blake hadn't known what happened, it meant he wasn't there, that someone else — suddenly, things were making better sense. God, and I'd put Blake through hell, my parents too. I nodded at my father. "I don't think he was even near the place," I said. "It had to be the other guys — Jordan Phelps and Todd Branton."

"Yes, probably both of them," said Ms. McKinnel. "Your son was driving — "

"Wait a minute," said my father. "He didn't have the car."

"Not the family car. It belonged to Ivan Buchko."

"Then Ivan must have been there," my mother said. "He can prove that Blake is innocent."

"Please." Ms. McKinnel held up her hand. "Young Buchko wasn't with him. If you'll just let me explain. Your son instructed me to tell you what he did that night."

"Yes. Go ahead," said my father.

"There was a football party. At Fentons' place, the parents were away. Blake said that he went there for a while, but he didn't feel like partying. How did he put it? 'I didn't seem to fit in anymore — didn't want to fit in.'"

Good, I thought, good for him. He shouldn't want to hang with guys like that.

"As he was leaving, Ivan Buchko threw him his keys, told him to drive around till he was feeling better. On the way out, he bumped into Vaughn Foster. Or Vaughn bumped him, stumbled against him on the stairs — he'd been drinking, said something about having a hot date that night. Blake told him he'd better not be driving and left the house. He had the impression that Foster was looking for someone at the party. A few minutes later he was sitting outside in the car when he saw Foster drive off. No one else in the car. Your son decided to follow him."

"Why would he do that?" my mother asked. "Was he going to stop him from driving drunk?"

Ms. McKinnel tucked a strand of hair behind her ear. "No, I don't think that was it. I think he wanted to see who Foster's hot date was going to be. He was a bit embarrassed about this, but he had an idea as to who it might be. He'd seen the Foster boy chatting up a particular girl in the halls at school. So he followed along behind, saw him stop outside Mr. Sub and honk his horn. A girl came running out to Foster's car, and he knew her right away — Anna Big Sky. When they pulled away, your son followed them, stayed behind them to the edge of town. He figured they were probably going out to the Goring farm."

"Why the Goring farm?" my father asked.

I knew why. "The Gorings move south as soon as they get the crops off."

My father looked perplexed. I had to tell him all of it.

"They have this long driveway between two lines of poplars. It's where everybody goes to make out."

My mother reached across my father and jabbed my thigh. "How do you know this?"

"Kids talk at school. Everybody knows it." I wanted her attention back on Ms. McKinnel and turned to the lawyer. "Blake didn't follow them outside of town?"

Ms. McKinnel shook her head. "He said he was feeling like a dork — I believe that was the term he used — said it was none of his business what they did."

Yes, I could hear him saying that.

My father was running his index finger over his right ear. "Exactly where is this leading?" he asked.

"Your son didn't feel like going back to the party yet. He drove around for quite a while, listening to music. For about an hour, he thinks." Ms. McKinnel paused. I could see a Gourami in the fish tank behind her head. It looked as if it was about to take a slice out of her left ear. "He was driving north on Main Street, out toward the overpass when he saw a silver Camry coming into town. It was the Foster car, but young Foster wasn't driving. He was in the passenger seat. Jordan Phelps was behind the wheel. There was no sign of Anna Big Sky — but there was another car right behind it and when that car passed him he saw the driver's face. It was Todd Branton. No sign of Anna there either."

"What did he do?" My father glanced at me when I spoke, but turned quickly back to Ms. McKinnel.

"He took a drive out to the Goring farm. There was one car way down at the end of the lane. A couple necking. He didn't recognize them."

"Why didn't he go after the other guys?" I asked. "Ask them what the heck was going on?" I felt a crazy urgency — as if somehow things could change and he could still save her.

"Be quiet, Blair." My father put out his hand, looked as if he might place it over my mouth.

"You must remember this was Saturday night. No one knew the girl was dead. Your brother said he felt uneasy, but that was the extent of it."

"Did he go out to the old McAuley place?"

"Blair!" This time his fingers did brush my lips.

"No, he didn't. He says he'd heard of it, but didn't know where it was."

"I don't understand," my mother said. "Our son hasn't done anything wrong. Why are the police holding him?"

She sounded dense, I know, but she was just worked up.

"How did he get involved?" my father asked, his words like heavy footsteps on the heels of my mother's question.

"When he heard of Anna's death, he had his suspicions, of course, but he didn't go to the police. He went to Vaughn Foster instead, tried to get him to say what had happened. The boy wouldn't tell him anything. Neither would the other two." Ms. McKinnel had been leaning toward us, her hands flat on her desk, but now she sank back into her chair. A Black Molly was swimming just above her head, circling slowly, like something ominous, waiting. "I think, perhaps, your son has a misguided sense of loyalty to his friends. I understand they all played football together. Perhaps that's why he decided to give them a break, said he wasn't going to turn them in, it would be better for them if they went to the police themselves."

Just like I told him, I thought. The same thing exactly. And look where it got him.

"He even gave them a deadline — Saturday at supper time — or he would do it for them. But then the police got a tip on Friday afternoon, and they didn't get the chance."

I wondered if my parents were glaring at me, but I didn't look to see.

I was relieved when Ms. McKinnel kept talking. "Blake thinks — and I tend to agree with him — that that was when they decided to lay the blame on him. When the police were called in before Saturday."

Lord, I thought, because I couldn't wait — wouldn't wait. I was so damned sure of myself I had to phone the tip line no matter how he argued. If only he had told me what was going on. If only I had figured — my mother was saying something.

" — have to be some kind of evidence? They're not going to take the word of three boys, are they?"

"Certainly not. The police have photographed the scene where she was beaten, they have impressions of the footprints found there, of the tire tracks. They impounded the Foster car. I'm sure they'll be looking at the tires on the other cars — Buchko's and Branton's. They've been examining everything for any clues as to who might have been there. I don't think they're going to find any sign of your son, Mrs. Russell."

"Then we can take him home after the hearing?" It was the question she had asked before, the words almost identical, and I wanted to hug her, tell her I was sorry, make it all disappear.

"I don't know about that. It will depend on what the boys say. One of them may change his story. They're not exactly hardened criminals — the Foster boy was fined once for having open liquor in a vehicle, but that's it. Perhaps, the pressure will get to them — I don't know. You can't count on it."

My mother sat with her hands between her knees as if that might keep them warm, but now she raised them, her fingers falling together as they would in prayer. When she looked down and saw them wavering there before her face, she quickly dropped them to her lap. I looked away. "It doesn't seem fair," she said, "that he should have to wait."

"It's the law, I guess," my father said. I couldn't bear to have them look at me. He laid his right hand on hers, gave it a quick pat. Seemed to recognize the uselessness of a pat. "Ms. McKinnel, do the police know what happened out there — at the McAuley place — who beat the girl?"

"That would be mere conjecture on my part."

"Does anyone know why they did it?"

"Your son said he thought Foster liked the girl, but he'd heard racist comments from the other two. He couldn't say more than that."

But I could.

All I had to do was close my eyes, and right now I would see Anna Big Sky striding toward Jordan Phelps, hear her calling him, "Asshole," her fist slamming his shoulder, her knee catching him in the crotch, and then she was pulling Amber free and the two of them were running down the hall.

"It would help," said Ms. McKinnel, "if we could establish some connection between the other boys and the Big Sky girl. Something more specific than racist comments."

"I can help," I said. "Jordan Phelps was mad as hell at her. She called him an asshole, kneed him in the — groin."

"This is something you heard about?"

"I was there."

"You're not just saying this? To help your brother?"

"No, I swear. I saw it happen."

"Can anyone corroborate what you say?"

"Amber Saunders. She was there too."

Ms. McKinnel wrote down the name. "This is vital information. I wish you'd told me sooner. Is there anything else that might be of help?"

There was nothing more I could tell her, except about the guys spouting racist comments in the shower. I wanted to talk to my brother.

~~~

The funeral for Anna Big Sky was held that afternoon in Assiniboia, there being no place in Wood Mountain big enough to hold the number of people expected to attend. Assiniboia was a hundred kilometres from Palliser, but the highway hotline reported that the roads were clear, there hadn't been much snow in the south. I pleaded with my parents to let me go, told them I could catch a ride with Ivan Buchko. My father wondered if I should be at my brother's remand hearing, but I argued that I had to go to Anna's funeral, that Blake would go himself if he only had the chance. My mother looked at me and tried to smile. "Under the circumstances," she said, "I think he'll understand."

There must have been half a dozen cars leaving the school at noon that day for the drive south on number two. Ivan had three girls from the student council riding with him, but he said there was lots of room for me. When I came out to the crescent in front of the school, the three girls, who were all in grade twelve, were clustered around his Ford, talking, but they shut up when they saw me coming. And stood looking at me as if I had an extra nostril in the middle of my forehead. At least I got to sit up front with Ivan. Still, I could feel them staring at me from behind. For a while, the back seat was filled with talk about how awful it was to die so young, how stupid those boys were to think they could get away with anything like this, but by the time the road began to rise into the hills south of town the conversation had petered out to the occasional brief comment about school or another nervous remark about funerals. I was afraid I knew what was coming next.

Finally, the girl directly behind me, Andrea, the yearbook editor, tapped me on the shoulder. "Considering the situation and all," she said, "it's good of you to go."

I suppose I could have grunted some noncommittal reply, but I had to get it out. "What do you mean?"

"You know," she said, "when your brother's one of the guys who did it."

I swung around in my seat, glared at her until she drew back into the corner of the car.

"My brother," I said, "had nothing to do with it. Absolutely nothing." That might be the truth — I hoped it was. "He's the one who tried to get the others to confess. You'll see. There'll be a trial, and then everybody's going to know what really happened."

I never should have phoned that Crime Stoppers line, I was such an idiot, now they all had it wrong about my brother, and I couldn't do a thing but let them wait for the trial — and who knew how long it would be before they'd learn the truth? What he said was the truth, wasn't it? It just had to be.

There wasn't much conversation after that, Ivan's radio droning on, the songs an empty murmur above the moan of tires on pavement.

I sat hunched against the door, staring out the window. The road carved its way up and around bare hills that looked dead and brown, no variation except for an occasional patch of dirty snow, the odd stagnant slough. Hardly any trees. A grey barn collapsing beside a weathered stack of hay, an old combine abandoned on a hilltop. From another, higher, hill, I could see far in the west a huge spread of water, its surface like slate, as drab as the sky. It had to be Old Wives Lake, and I couldn't help but think of a story from the distant past, more killing, the old native women circling their carts, making camp for the night, knowing the enemy would attack at dawn. They lit many campfires, made enough commotion for a whole tribe, gave all the young a chance to steal away in the dark. When the Blackfoot struck the next morning, they found only old wives, grandmothers, they killed them all.

The wives were Cree though, Anna was Sioux. I'd read her obituary in the paper, had cut it out, slipped it inside the pocket of my good jacket. Her father was dead — "predeceased by her father" was what the paper said. She had an older sister, a mother and a grandmother on the reserve near Wood Mountain, a grandmother and grandfather in Palliser, the ones she lived with while she went to school. Ivan told me that her grandpa worked at the potash plant east of Palliser. The obituary said that Anna loved her family more than anything, but that she liked sports and school, wanted to go to university.

The sky seemed lower now and darker, clouds moving slowly overhead, though there was no wind, the tall grass around the fence posts motionless. All we needed now was freezing rain; it'd be a perfect day for a funeral.

When we got to Assiniboia, the church was nearly full, the pews at the back jammed with kids from school. Ivan and I squeezed into the last row. I could see a lot of people I didn't know in the forward rows, many of them natives, a few with their hair tied in braids. Except for that and their darker skin, they looked pretty much like the rest of us. Right behind them, all crowded into the same row, were the girls from Anna's volleyball team and Mrs. Kennedy, their coach. Mr. Teale, the principal, was in the next row, and Mr. Hilton too, the guidance counsellor. The first few rows were empty, and right in front of them was Anna's coffin.

I tried not to look at it, but then I saw her picture on the coffin, and a bunch of flowers. It was okay, the coffin was closed. Her school picture — the Josten's photographer took everybody's picture in the fall, so it was her graduation photograph, and she was never going to graduate.

I looked down. The pew in front of me, whorled figures at rest in the grain of the wood.

When the minister asked us all to stand, I tried not to stare toward the aisle. Two men in black suits walked slowly to the front of the church and turned around, one of them motioning to the reserved seats. They were followed by three women, also in black, two of whom were guiding an older woman who walked between them with short, precise steps. Anna's sister and her mother, I thought, helping her grandma. Right behind them must have been her other grandparents, both of them with black, black hair, their faces looking strained and tired. Otherwise, they seemed no older than my parents. A dozen more in the procession, and then everyone was seated and the service underway.

It was a lot like you'd expect. We sang "Amazing Grace" and "Rock of Ages," listened to some scripture and the homily. When the minister mentioned Anna's name though, his tone was so impersonal you had to guess he'd probably never met her. Then he asked Yvonne Big Sky to speak about her sister. Yvonne walked quickly to the lectern, pulled a paper from her pocket — she was wearing a black blazer over a white blouse, the paper in the inside pocket of the blazer — she spread the paper in front of her. She looked a bit like Anna, high cheekbones and handsome eyes, but she wasn't as tall.

The microphone attached to the lectern was above her head, and she took it in one hand and lowered it towards her mouth. I could see then that she was biting her lower lip.

There was a long pause before she spoke.

"My sister was a remarkable person. Even when she was a little girl, Anna had big ambitions. She said some day she was going to be a teacher. She wanted to help her people."

The woman's lip was quivering, and I wondered, how can she get through this when it's for her own sister?

"Everybody knew Anna could be serious, but she was lots of fun too. She always liked to sing. She used to make up her own songs." Yvonne Big Sky paused, took a deep breath. Another breath. "Not her own songs. Her own words for other people's songs. Funny words. Once, when Mom overcooked the roast, she sang Kris Kristofferson. 'Help me make it through the meat.' She liked to . . . tease. She . . . she . . ." Anna's sister closed her eyes. When she opened them, they were full of tears. "I'm sorry," she said. "I can't do this." She hurried back to the seat beside her grandma. I could hear weeping from the front of the church now where Anna's relatives were seated, and farther back some of the girls on the school volleyball team began to cry.

The next thing I knew, the minister was reading scripture.

"O God, whose days are without end, and whose mercies cannot be numbered: Make us, we beseech thee, deeply sensible of the shortness and uncertainty of human life . . ."

I'm not sure what came after that. I could hardly make out the grain in the pew in front of me.

On the drive back to Palliser, I kept thinking that's the way it ought to be. People crying, letting their grief show, not like when my uncle died, the whole family gritting their teeth, keeping quiet as if it was some kind of shame to cry. When I get home, I thought, I'm going down to that jail and tell Blake exactly what it was like at Anna's funeral.

Yeah, and there was so much more we had to talk about. I wanted to see him. Needed desperately to talk to him.

But, as I learned when I got home, I would never have the chance.

ELEVEN

My brother's funeral was held on Friday at St. David's Church in Palliser, my father's church, but the Reverend Wallace Garner from St. Timothy's on the east side of town volunteered to take the service. A lot of it was just a blur, I was still in such a shock, and I couldn't seem to cry for my brother. Which was crazy. I felt like crying, wanted to cry. My father was on the other side of my mother, I remember that, each of us holding one of her hands as we sat in the first pew, my cousins, aunts and uncles in the rows behind us, but when the service began she removed her hands from ours, picked up the *Book of Common Prayer* — it was the one she'd chosen, wanting the more stately language of the past — and turned to the funeral liturgy.

When we'd come down the aisle a few minutes earlier, the three of us walking together, supporting my mother, or so I thought — I didn't yet know how strong she was — and leading the procession of relatives, I had glanced up from where my mother held my arm and been surprised to see that the church was full. Many of the parish congregation were there, as one might expect, and Evan Morgan, I knew I could count on him, but I also saw quite a few other kids from my grade nine classes, many more that I knew were seniors, and then, filling the better part of three rows, Coach Conley and the football team.

Except, of course, for the three who'd been remanded to the youth facility in Regina. Everything had changed with my brother's death.

Vaughn Foster began to talk as soon as he learned that Blake was dead. He said he was out there with Anna Big Sky, the other car had hemmed him in, he had no idea who it was, didn't want any part of what they might do. When he saw it was Jordan Phelps and Todd Branton, he knew it was going to be bad.

After that, Todd Branton couldn't wait to lay the blame on Jordan. He said it was his car, but Jordan had been driving, they'd followed the Foster car all right, but he thought they were just going to have some fun with Anna, put a scare into her, sure he'd helped Vaughn Foster hold her, but only after Jordan had grabbed her and she'd slugged him one. Then Jordan had started hitting her, hammering her in the face, and he had let her go. So had Vaughn a minute later, but Jordan kept hitting her, striking her even as she fell. They had both seized him then, but he kicked her twice while she lay on the ground. When she didn't move, Jordan had said they were in this together, they were all guilty, they had to keep it quiet or the three of them were finished, there was a way they could show they were going to stick together, something they could do together. Todd said he didn't want to do it, of course, but what choice did he have? Once Vaughn agreed to do it, he had to do it too.

They were guilty, yes, but they were still alive.

Vaughn Foster told a somewhat different story. He didn't know what made him hold her, but she'd slugged Jordan when he reached for her. Then she'd called Jordan an asshole and he'd started hitting her. Vaughn claimed that he'd been the first to let her go, that he was the one who didn't want to piss on the girl. It wasn't their fault, they both agreed on that; Jordan Phelps was the one responsible and, besides, everybody was drunk.

I still hadn't cried for my brother. It was his funeral, sure, but I kept thinking of Anna Big Sky.

Regaining consciousness under that chill October sky, she wonders where she is — the clothes she wears, the snow beneath her, everything soaked with urine. Somehow she climbs to her feet, her legs barely holding her weight, her eyes so swollen from the beating that she can hardly see. Pale grasses like ghosts moving slowly over the snow. Brush and deadfall, the dark shadows of broken maples like warnings scrawled upon the drifts, but somewhere out there, far beyond the trees, she sees a light. Shivering now, her whole body beginning to shake, she knows that distant light is the only hope she has. Her clothes already begin to stiffen with the cold.

The bastards, the dirty bastards. Jordan Phelps wanting his revenge because Anna had the nerve to take him on and show him up for what he was. Branton along for the ride, not just to put a scare into her, but because he'd do whatever Jordan wanted, yeah, that was true, he'd follow Jordan anywhere. And Vaughn Foster, I wasn't sure about him. He might have gone along with it, but Anna liked him, and I think he liked her too. Maybe he was just another victim. I guess I'd never know.

She sets off toward the light, her feet slipping on stones and fallen branches. She stumbles, sinks to her knees, forces herself to rise again. Pushes on, through the brush and fallen trees. Branches lash across her face, cut her battered cheeks. She raises a hand before her eyes, blunders on, breath sharp in her throat.

She bounces off a tree, almost goes down again, but she keeps her feet moving, keeps them under her, pushes a branch away from her face, breaks through the line of trees, and the whole prairie lies before her, snow like a frayed and dirty sheet dropped upon the stubble field. She wavers above her aching legs. The light is straight ahead, warmth and safety waiting there, but she can't stop the shaking.

She begins to walk again, the crust of snow clawing at her feet, trying to pull her down, but she keeps dragging one foot around, putting it in front of the other. She trips on something in the snow. Falls. Lies there a moment, the snow so soft beneath her. But there's a light ahead somewhere; she knows she has to reach it. She gets her legs beneath her, crouches until her legs have the strength to lift her. Yes, the light is there.

She starts off again, leaning to her right — she can't seem to help it — the light is side-stepping away from her. She pauses, shakes her head, goes straight toward it, but it's slipping off again. She knows she's staggering. Stops, her body shuddering, her hands quaking at her sides. She sinks into the snow.

" — the kind of kid who always tried to do his best." Coach Conley was delivering my brother's eulogy. My parents, I suddenly noticed, were gazing at him as if every breath they took came straight from him. "Blake did not believe in giving up. I remember when he was in grade ten the Lightning football team was not the power it's been the last two years. One Saturday afternoon, we were down by three touchdowns at halftime. The boys are all lying on the sidelines, chewing on oranges, wondering just how bad the score is going to be by the final whistle, wishing they could get it over with and go home right now, and this grade ten kid stands up, tells everybody he doesn't know if they can win this game, but one thing he does know is that none of them are quitters, if they put their hearts back into it and all pull together, sure as shooting they can win the second half. It's obvious the kid believes this himself, and pretty soon the other guys are starting to believe right along with him. They do outscore the other team the rest of the way, darn near pull out the victory. Because Blake Russell believed in them and in himself."

Coach Conley paused, gazed out above the microphone in the chancel, gazed down at us. My parents stared back at him, their faces glowing, as if they could see my brother standing there beside him.

"Like I said, this was a kid who tried to do his best. He didn't always succeed, but you knew he'd always try. And it's true sometimes he made mistakes. He was human — just like the rest of us. But in all my years of coaching, I've seldom seen a boy with the sense of responsibility that he had." Both my parents were crying now, but it was crazy — I was too damned rational to cry. Even then I was wondering if maybe Coach was getting kind of schmaltzy here, but the thing about it was, he pretty much had it right.

"When Blake made a mistake," Coach continued, "he never forgot it. That was why we picked him for quarterback even though we knew he wasn't the best athlete on the team. He might make a mistake, throw a pass, say, when he should have grounded the ball, but he was never going to make that same mistake again. That's a good quality all right, but I'd have to say it's a heavy burden too. When Blake Russell did something wrong, I don't believe he ever forgave himself."

There was a sudden noise, not much louder than a sigh, something like a gasp and moan combined, a stunted cry of pain. I didn't have to look at either of my parents to know they turned toward me.

Coach Conley was going on about the kind of student my brother was, but his words were running together now, his hands dissolving on the lectern, his face a blur, his shoulders melting down, collapsing, and mine were shaking; I was digging at my eyes, the tears streaming for my brother.

~·~·~

After the relatives had all left for home, driving back to Saskatoon and Estevan, I helped my parents gather up the dishes, collect uneaten food in plastic bags and take them downstairs to the freezer. We stuffed all the dishes we could into the dishwasher, then with my mother washing, my father and I drying and putting things away, we finished off the other dishes, hardly saying a word, the washer whirring mournfully beneath the counter. I thought that if anybody got started, we might have to talk about the way my brother died, and I knew it was too soon for that. I couldn't bear it yet. As soon as I'd set the last glass in the buffet, I went up to bed.

The room across the hall from mine was empty. It always would be now.

Lying in bed, I felt chilly, even with a comforter pulled over my blankets. The room was somewhat brighter than usual, the blind over my desk pulled just halfway down. I stared at the ceiling, the shadow above my bed dark and ominous, shivers rocking my spine. It was nothing but the shadow of the lighting fixture, but on the stippled ceiling of my bedroom it looked like a body lying on snow. If it had begun to move, crawling, staggering to its feet, I wouldn't have been surprised.

Anna, I thought, oh Anna, you never had a chance. Those rotten bastards never gave you a chance. You didn't know it, Anna, but I loved you, I would have done anything — no, that was craziness. I liked her because she always spoke to me, admired her for her nerve, felt sorry for the way she'd suffered, but that was not the same as love. I hardly knew her.

My brother was the one I loved.

My brother who was dead, dead and gone forever.

I hadn't found a way to forgive him. And he couldn't forgive himself.

Some time later I crawled out of bed and lowered the blind to the sill. Before I pulled it down, I stared a moment at the street outside. Though the traffic had worn the snow away, the whole street shimmered, pavement transformed to ice by the spare glow of moonlight. It was the street where we used to gather after school, a whole gang of kids, choosing sides for road hockey. My brother always picked me early so I wouldn't be the last one taken.

～～～

"We need to talk," my father said, coming into my room on Tuesday night. I'd gone back to school that day, was at my desk now, trying to scratch out a long enough descriptive paragraph to satisfy my English teacher.

"I'm kind of busy writing," I said. "Got a paragraph that's due tomorrow morning."

"I've been standing at your door — must be nearly five minutes. Your pen hasn't moved."

"I'm thinking."

"Maybe you need a break."

I heard his feet pad across the floor, heard springs squeak. Knew he was sitting on the bed beside my desk. I kept my eyes on the sheet of foolscap, half a dozen lines scrawled at the top of the page.

"Before your brother died," he said, his voice not quite his own when he pronounced the word 'died', "it was obvious something had gone wrong between the two of you. You were barely talking. You've been in a deep funk ever since."

Get off my case, I thought, and suddenly I felt like hurting him. "Naturally," I snapped. "My brother's dead." I felt sorry at once, turned to look at him, shaking my head, hoping he would take it for apology.

Sitting there on my bed, the mattress sunk below the level of my chair, he looked withered, older than his years.

"I don't want to argue with you, Blair, but I think there's something there you need to talk about."

He was studying my face, and I tried not to blink.

You really want to hear this, I thought. What your son did to Amber, I could tell you that. Really hurt you. Yeah, might as well shove a knife between your ribs.

"What about it, Blair?"

I shook my head. Why couldn't he just leave me alone?

"Blair?" He wasn't going to quit. Leaning toward me, his right hand out as if he expected me to drop an offering in it, looking so pathetic.

"Okay," I said. "Okay! There was something between us. I was mad as hell at him. Because of something he'd done."

My father didn't look surprised — just more tired than usual — and I knew I'd gone too far already. I didn't want this leading to the truth.

"Don't clam up now."

"It wasn't all that serious, but . . . well, it really got to me." He was still leaning toward me, wanting more. Not serious, hell, another bloody lie, I was through lying. I'd tell him as much as he could handle. "Blake did something that was really stupid. I promised him I'd never tell anybody."

"You need to tell me, Blair. For your own sake."

"No, I don't."

"You do." He stood up, stepped toward my chair. "Right now. I'm not leaving till you do."

"You really want to know? You'll be sorry." He nodded. I had to tell him, there was no other way to get him out of here. "That night Blake came home so drunk, he wasn't the only one like that. A bunch of them were drunk, a girl too, Amber Saunders. She passed out on Fosters' lawn, and those guys — " My voice was shaking now. " — it wasn't Blake's idea, it was Jordan Phelps' — they all stood there and . . . they peed on her."

My father sat down, suddenly. He looked as if I'd hit him.

"Blake was sick about it. I said I wouldn't tell you." I took a deep breath, tried not to sob. "When Anna died — where she was beat up, the snow was all yellow. They'd done the same thing. That's why I thought it was Blake. But I was wrong. He'd never do anything like that again."

My father had tears in his eyes. "I see," he said. "That's what was going on." I could barely hear him.

"I wasn't supposed to tell. I promised." And then I broke down, sobbing like a fool. I'd betrayed my bother.

"The two of you," he said, his voice louder now, "you were both going through hell."

"Yeah."

He stood up again, bent toward me and gave me an awkward hug in my chair. "You were right to tell, Blair. Some things need saying, or they just eat away inside."

I thought he was finished, but he sat back down, taking his weight on his hands, and pushed himself across the bed until he was leaning against the wall. "I know you loved your brother."

"Of course, I did!" Was he going to stay here all night and make stupid comments?

"Yes." He looked almost relaxed with his back resting on the wall. His eyelids slowly closed. "The thing is, I think you're still angry with him."

"Maybe I am." I was surprised at his statement, surprised at my response.

His eyes were still shut, but he had more to say. "Judge not, and ye shall not be judged; condemn not, and ye shall not be condemned." His eyes flicked open, held me like spotlights on a deer. "Forgive, and ye shall be forgiven."

"I don't think I believe that stuff anymore." I said it, angered by the way he was always going to the Bible now, but I might have been afraid that he was right. I wiped my eyes with the back of my hand.

My father looked hurt. "It's been serving people well for centuries, advice on how to conduct our affairs, how to live. It's been good enough for more brilliant people than we can imagine, people a lot smarter than we'll ever be."

There was something in what he said, I know, but his Bible-spouting inflamed me. I wanted to take him on. "How come every time you turn around they're changing what it says?"

"What do you mean?"

"There's the King James Version, the New Revised Version, the Jerusalem Bible, the Good News Bible. I don't know how many others."

"The language might change a bit, they make the same point."

"How do we know it isn't all a load of crap? Every version of it pure bullshit."

"Blair! You're angry. You don't know what you're saying." He was rigid against the wall, trying to hold his temper.

"I know exactly what I'm saying. If God had any power at all, he would've kept Blake alive."

"Don't blame God!" he said, his voice rising as he heaved himself across the bed. "Don't you dare blame God!" He grabbed me by the hand, squeezed it tight. "And don't blame yourself. You mustn't do that." His grip like pliers on my fingers.

I felt tears stinging my eyes again.

He noticed, dropped my hand at once. "I didn't mean to hurt you."

I could still feel the pressure of his fingers, but it wasn't that. He'd squeezed my hand exactly the way that Blake had squeezed it, the last time I'd seen him.

If I didn't say something, I knew I was going to cry again, but I'd done enough of that already, crying for Blake, crying for myself. "Whose fault is it then?"

My father shrugged. Hesitated, ducked his head. Then he said something that surprised me, something I'd often heard from mouthy kids spouting off at school, something I never thought I'd hear from him. "Shit happens. It gets smeared everywhere. It's just part of life. What matters is that we figure out a way to handle it." He reached for me again, put his arms around me, held me, my head buried against his chest.

If he looked he would see that my cheek was wet, but he wasn't going to hear me crying any more. I let him hold me till I was certain my voice wouldn't waver when I spoke.

"I want to see where he died," I said.

～～～

After my father talked to him — I have no idea what he said to convince him, or even if it was difficult — Mr. Hammond agreed to show us around. It's still the only time in my life I've ridden in a cop car. My father sat in the passenger seat, and I was in the back, a Plexiglas screen separating me from the front seat and the driver. My mother chose to stay at home. She said there was nothing there she needed to see. Or wanted to see.

We drove through the city parking lot, past sites reserved for the mayor, the chief of police, the city commissioner, entered the police station through a huge grey door, which rose before us exactly like the automatic door in our garage at home. When Mr. Hammond shut the engine off, I glanced out the car's rear window, the door dropping closed behind us. Mr. Hammond got out of the car and opened the back door for me.

"Blake came down to the station himself," he said, "through the front door, but this is where they brought the others in. It's a secure bay."

I looked around me. Drab blank walls without a window, a wire cage full of bicycles, probably stolen, bikes that had somehow been recovered, another cage with three cases of beer locked inside it. Mr. Hammond saw me looking at the beer. "Evidence," he said, but offered no further explanation. It was all new to me. When I'd been down to see Blake, I'd come through the street entrance with Ms. McKinnel.

Mr. Hammond led us to a metal door, punched four numbers into a key pad, swung the door open, motioned for us to enter. When I hesitated, my father stepped into the station first. Following behind him now, I saw a brightly lit hall, the kind you might find in any office building. It didn't seem like a jail.

I felt foolish, holding back like that, and turned to Mr. Hammond. "Which way's the basement?"

He looked puzzled. "You want to see the basement?"

"Aren't the cells down there?"

"No. Cells are this way." He must have seen my ears begin to burn because he quickly added, "I guess in the old building they were in the basement. Before my time. I dare say, it wasn't the best place for a lockup."

Was I thinking about a dungeon? Was that what it was? Stone walls and darkness, dank smells, prisoners clinging to iron bars.

We walked along the hall and passed a central desk, a clerk doing paperwork, a monitor on a shelf in front of him. Mr. Hammond led us through a doorway, its metal door wide open. I noticed a video camera mounted high on the wall beyond the door.

"No one in the cells today," Mr. Hammond said. "That's the case a lot of the time." He motioned to another open door. "We can take a look at a cell if you like. They're all the same."

The three of us stood a moment in the empty hall. I saw my father turn to Mr. Hammond and raise his eyebrows.

"Yes, well," he said, "I guess you might say this is where it started." He took half a dozen steps down the hall and pointed to another sliding door. "Right here." So that was the door he'd hit.

We already knew what had happened.

Mr. Hammond had come over to the house himself to tell us the story, to make sure we got the details straight. I remembered how hard it was for him, crushing his cap in his hand, seated in our living room on the same chair where he'd sat for my parents' open house at Epiphany, my mother sobbing on the couch, but, although he glanced more than once toward our front door, he made no attempt to leave until he was sure he'd answered all my parents' questions.

I stared at the cell door. Metal hard and solid as a wall, the kind of thing you might expect to see on a bunker in a bomb shelter. We were standing where he had stood. I knew I could close my eyes and see it happen.

The guys are wearing handcuffs as two officers escort them down the hall. They all walk slowly, as if they'd prefer to remain in their individual cells rather than have to face a judge together. My brother's in the lead, Jordan Phelps a step or two behind him. Vaughn Foster and Todd Branton are even farther back. They shuffle along, seem to dawdle until an officer says, "Move along, eh. We're not going to a picnic."

That's when Jordan Phelps speaks, his voice so quiet only one of the men is close enough to catch the words. "Bastard, you're the one who killed her."

But as he speaks, he lunges at my brother, ramming him from behind, his shoulder driving Blake into the metal door. Blake's head slams against the door, snaps back. Before anyone can catch him, he falls over backwards, landing hard, his head bouncing on the floor.

One of the officers shoves Jordan aside, the other pulls Blake to his feet, asks if he's okay. Blake nods his head, and they lead him down the hall to face the judge. After that, he doesn't speak to anyone.

I was staring at the door. It was solid metal, not a bar on it. A window so thick, you suspected even a brick wouldn't crack it.

Mr. Hammond must have noticed me. "It's a sliding door," he said. "Once it's shut, nothing budges it but us."

I had to ask the question. "Is this the cell where he — ?" But I couldn't say it.

Mr. Hammond frowned. He walked down the hall and nodded toward an open door.

We stepped through the doorway. There were no bars anywhere; the cell was made of concrete. A stainless steel toilet on the far wall, a sink attached to it, also stainless steel. There was no toilet seat, I noted, and no handles, the water in both sink and toilet controlled by pressing buttons. The bed was in the corner, but there was no bed frame. The mattress, which looked thin, lay on what seemed to be a shelf of solid steel. The whole place cold and sterile. I couldn't imagine spending a single night here.

"Not much to see," said Mr. Hammond. He looked uncomfortable. "It's basically your bare room."

My father was already backing out the door, but I was staring at the vent on the wall above the sink. I had to be sure. "This is . . . where he did it?"

Mr. Hammond took a deep breath, let it slowly out. "He must've been depressed as hell. That, and the knock on the head, maybe. We had his shoe laces, his belt, but he took off his shirt, ripped it into strips. Knotted them together, tied a noose in one end." Mr. Hammond was talking faster now; he'd already told us what had happened, but he couldn't seem to stop himself. "Only way he could've reached the vent would be by standing on the sink there. Somehow he got his line threaded through the vent. Clerk at the desk checks the cells on a regular schedule, saw him hanging there. Lord, he was still warm when they got to him, but they couldn't bring him back."

Right here was where it happened — because I lost my patience with him, because I wouldn't wait and turned the others in. Because Jordan Phelps figured Blake had ratted on him and labelled Blake the killer.

I was leaning on the door, the metal hard and chill beneath my palm, my forehead resting on what seemed a slab of ice, when I felt my father's hand fall upon my shoulder. He pulled me to him then and wrapped me in his arms. A while after that I heard his voice behind me.

"Thanks, Ham," he said. "I don't know if it will help, but I think we've seen enough."

A few minutes later, Mr. Hammond drove us home.

∽·∽·∽

Another night of staring at the ceiling, my legs, my arms taut as the metal frame on the bed.

I'd gone through everything — well, almost everything — tried to keep it all in order, see it as it happened. For three years after Blake's death, my parents went about their business the same as usual, but they moved as if they were hypnotized, as if they'd been told what was expected of them, but they couldn't quite get it right. For a while my father talked about leaving the Diocese of Qu'Appelle and applying for a transfer to Rupertsland, but my mother wouldn't think of moving east to Winnipeg. This was our home, she said, we weren't going to leave it.

Sometimes in the evening when I walked by my father's den, I'd see him hunched over his desk and wonder if he'd been crying. If he did cry, he made sure I never heard him, never saw his tears. Once or twice, when he was conducting a funeral I'd hear him hesitate in the middle of his homily, and I'd think that he was struggling to control his feelings, but I couldn't be sure. He kept going because he had his faith to keep him going. So did my mother.

I never saw her cry but once after my brother's funeral. Late one evening they were at the dining room table, the last time my father talked about a transfer. "No," she said, "we're staying here." They'd done nothing wrong, she added, and neither had

Blake, not really. I suspect my father never told her about what had happened that night in Fosters' yard. I knew I'd never tell her. She had enough to deal with.

"Paul," she added after a pause, "you gave Blair some advice one night, and he took it — nothing wrong in that." Then she was crying, tears running down her cheeks, her chest heaving as she strained for breath. My father was so surprised, he didn't move for a minute. By the time he got to her, she had her handkerchief out, was dabbing at her eyes.

"It was me that was wrong," she said as he bent awkwardly towards her, putting his arms around her. "I was angry, crazy with anger. Pulling away from both of you. When we should have been talking. We might have been able to help Blake. To help each other."

"I didn't know what to do," I said. I thought I was going to cry too.

"Don't know why it is," my father said, "but sometimes it's easier to talk with people in the parish you hardly know." Although one arm was still around my mother, he reached toward me with his other hand and squeezed my shoulder. "Instead of the ones you love."

"Well," said my mother, "well. I guess that's sometimes how it is." She leaned against his chest for just a moment. "It's okay, Paul. I'm all right now."

When he released her, she reached for her coffee cup and took another swallow. "I was wrong about something else too," she said, "saying what I said that night. As if Indians didn't matter." She dumped what was left of her coffee into the sink. "I'm going up to bed. I've got things to do tomorrow."

The next morning, she started phoning people in the parish, proposing that on the second Sunday of every month it should be a parish project to bring donations for the food bank. That very day she went up to Canadian Tire and bought a huge rubber tub to hold whatever food was collected. I wondered if she was trying to ease her guilt, but I thought it best not to ask.

~~~

Amber Saunders came back to Palliser for the trial. Her family had moved to Saskatoon in the second semester of grade nine, Amber so cowed by events of that fall, by the talk that always swirled around her, she must've been glad to get away. At school in Palliser, it seemed, her eyes never left the floor. Even then, as green as I was, I was smart enough to see that whenever a guy or guys did something to a girl, it was usually the girl that everybody talked about, the girl whose reputation suffered. Saskatoon had to be a sanctuary after that. Still, when she gave her testimony, she was able to take the stand and describe how Anna Big Sky had angered Jordan Phelps. She didn't look at Jordan, but her voice never faltered.

It was a murder trial, of course, all three guys charged with first-degree murder, but the lawyers must've had some kind of weird influence on the jury, maybe the judge too, because even Jordan Phelps was convicted of nothing more than manslaughter. In his instructions to the jury the judge seemed to favour the boys who were alive over the girl who was dead. He emphasized that, except for a single liquor charge, these were boys with no criminal records, and they were all drunk, a fact that he said merited some consideration. He reminded members of the jury that the girl had been alive when they abandoned her, that she had, in fact, walked at least the distance of a city block.

After the verdict was announced, a Sioux chief from Wood Mountain spoke to the press on behalf of the Big Sky family. "This isn't justice," he said. "The family's outraged. It should be murder in the first degree. This one boy, he wanted to kill her, and that's exactly what they did. It was clearly racism."

I have no idea what the jury considered in their deliberations, but you had to feel for Anna's family. They couldn't help but be furious.

I thought it significant that, a week after the verdict, when the judge did the sentencing, he spoke of the repugnance of a crime so marked by brutality and degradation. The offenders, he said, were despicable cowards. He hadn't used those terms before, and I wondered if he was trying to make amends for the influence he'd had with his soft charge to the jury.

Jordan Phelps got the stiffest sentence, but it was only six and a half years. There was a series of letters to the paper after the sentencing, a big stink, in fact, but it didn't change a thing. Anna was still gone, and my brother too — his life snuffed out in an instant, and it's weird as hell, but for some reason I remembered that hawk in our backyard, falling on its prey, my mother startled, her hand at her mouth, suds dripping from her chin. There's the fate we face, I'm sure. It can strike at any time. Somehow we have to find a way to live with it.

"Forgive," my father said, "and ye shall be forgiven." Advice he found, I've long since learned, in the Gospel according to St Luke, and good advice it is, no doubt. Sometimes, though, it takes a while before you find a way to forgive yourself. When you know in your heart that if you weren't so pig-headed, if you'd sat down and talked to your brother, if you'd only levelled with him, things might have been different.

I'm older now than my brother when he died, and still I sometimes think I feel his hand gripping mine, his eyes imploring me, the moment already passing when I might have told him I understood his shame, his need to lie to me. The moment when I didn't speak.

Epilogue

I finished high school in Palliser. In grade ten I was still in such a turmoil that I refused to go out for football, but eventually I decided it was pointless punishing myself, and I played my last two years, cornerback on a pretty good team, a team that made it to the southern finals in my grade twelve year. After high school, I worked a year pumping gas at the Palliser Co-Op, living at home and saving as much money as I could, then went off to the University of Saskatchewan to study commerce.

It was during Frosh Week, at a campus rally in the bowl, that I first saw the girl I thought someday I might want to marry. Everybody was talking about a series of red "E"s that had appeared overnight on the windows of the Arts Building's upper floor. I remember an artsman commandeered the microphone, went on and on about what imbeciles the engineers always were. "Not much danger in a prank like that," he said. "They might fall from the top of the building, but there'd be no harm done as long as they managed to land on their heads."

A slim brunette was striding to the podium, streaks of red dyed in her hair and flaming under the noonday sun. There was something vaguely familiar about the way she walked, or, perhaps, the way she held her head. She went straight for the speaker, stepping over the legs of couples seated on the grass. The speaker saw her coming, liked what he saw, dipped his head in a preposterous bow and waved her toward the microphone.

She paused an instant before she spoke, and I noted her eyes, even from a distance, they seemed to be flashing with emotion.

"On this campus," she said, "artsmen and engineers have been exchanging insults for generations. Now, let me tell you, your average engineer isn't a bad sort. Just because he likes his beer and reads *The Red Eye*, don't make the mistake of thinking he's a redneck. He's too busy — stuck in class for thirty, forty hours a week. Your average artsman's not a bad sort either. The problem is the odd one who seldom goes to class. Hey, man, he's got his reading list, eh? Yes, and he flies through Jonathan Swift, head nodding all the way, but never a thought that he might be a yahoo too. Our problem here is the artsman whose brain is smaller than his mouth."

Cheers and boos from all across the bowl, and I was hooked already, knew I had to meet her, wanted to ask her out. Then I heard a guy behind me say, "That Saunders, she's got more guts than a slaughterhouse."

I wheeled around, saw two guys standing together, their Engineering jackets bright red in the sunlight.

"Who'd you say she is?"

"Amber Saunders."

"She's an Engineer?" I could hardly believe what I was hearing.

"Uh-huh, a chemical." Wow, I thought, this is really something.

"You don't think women should be engineers?"

I hadn't noticed her before, a dark-haired girl standing beside the engineers, her tan sweatshirt eclipsed by their red jackets. She'd taken a step toward me, and even with her brow furrowed, her jaw thrust forward, she was just about the cutest girl I'd ever seen. "Well," she said, "what about it?"

"Hey, women should be anything they want."

"You're sure of that, are you?" Her eyes were bright as sunlight on newly fallen snow.

"I was just surprised about Amber Saunders. I used to know her." And only a minute ago I'd had some goofy thought about wanting to take her out. Not Amber Saunders. Too many complications there.

"So women engineers are okay?"

The two in the red jackets were shaking their heads, laughing at her. "Come on, Owens," one of them said, "give the guy a break."

"Yeah, Owens," I said. "About the only thing better than women engineers is women who aren't afraid to speak their minds."

She was grinning at me now.

"So," I said, "you could really give this guy a break and let him take you out for coffee."

She was even cuter when she laughed.

We went for coffee. It turned out her name was Holly Owens and she was feisty all right, a chemical engineer herself, in second year, but within a month we were going steady.

～～～

The day I saw Amber Saunders walk through the campus crowd, I thought for an instant that there was something familiar about her, but eventually I realized I hadn't got it quite right. If the way she held herself struck me as vaguely familiar, it must have been because of how she walked, head up, shoulders back, her stride full of purpose. I'd seen that look before — Anna Big Sky swinging into action, going right for Jordan Phelps.

When I think of Anna now, I try not to dwell on the way she died, although it's never easy to get my mind beyond that trampled patch of snow. I like to remember how she'd pass me in the hall at school, my name on her lips, that sudden smile following as sure as the wine succeeds the wafer in my father's church, but what I like best is one time she did stop to talk. She said a few words only, but I keep them like souvenirs, love to take them out and polish them whenever I'm feeling low.

"Blair," she said, smiling as she always did, but this time she paused beside me. "You're number thirty-one, aren't you?"

I was so surprised that she would know my jersey number I could only nod my head.

"I saw you practising after school the other day." She laid her hand on my biceps, gave a quick squeeze. "I liked the way you stuck to that receiver. Kind of like Crazy Glue."

Before I could think of any response that wouldn't leave me sounding like a goof, she was on her way, heading for another class.

That's the memory I go back to again and again. Anna striding down the hall, me turned to watch her go, the other kids streaming by, no one shoving, no one bumping me because abruptly I'm transformed into a rock, substantial, solid, the water parting, flowing past, and nothing pushes me aside.

~·~·~

The guy at Mosaic Stadium must have been ten rows in front of me, but as soon as he stood up to harangue the Lions I felt apprehensive. Which was strange because he didn't look like anyone I knew.

The guy was big — must've been well over six-feet tall — with a lean torso and arms like a weight-lifter, and he moved with the agility of an athlete, hopping onto his seat between plays, both arms in the air, middle fingers raised for all to see, his hands swinging down a minute later, jabbing at number thirty-six who'd made the mistake of glancing over his shoulder, distracted, I suppose, by the shouts behind him. Before every play the fan hopped nimbly down and took his seat, but the second the play was finished he was up again, yelling at the one Lion who'd noticed him.

Though I couldn't hear him with all the crowd noise, I felt a tightening in the muscles of my neck. I tried to watch the action on the field, but my eyes were always coming back to him. There was something about the easy way he moved.

When play stopped at the three-minute mark, he pushed his way out to the aisle, ran down the steps to the rail and leaned toward the Lion bench. He hollered something I couldn't hear, and number thirty-six laughed and pointed to the scoreboard. The guy in the stands looked as if he'd been slapped. The Riders were down by ten points, but that didn't seem to mean a thing to him. He flung himself against the rail, shaking his fist, waving with his other hand for the player to come on up and fight. Before long, half a dozen other guys in the front row were joining in, backing him up, all of them behaving like jerks, challenging the Lions to fight.

I suppose that's when I should have known.

He stayed at the rail for the game's final minutes, squatting down during the action so he wouldn't block someone's view and attract a security guard, hurling himself against the rail between plays, leaning as far out and over as he could, both hands outstretched, palms up, fingers beckoning. Four of the Lions were turned toward him now, yapping back up at him, making the same kind of beckoning motions, urging him to come down and fight.

There was a sudden break in the noise and I heard him yell, "Pussies! You're all a bunch of pussies!"

I sat down. Jammed my hands between my knees. The Riders completed a long pass on the next play, but I didn't care.

No matter how hard I clamped my knees together, I couldn't stop the shaking. I felt the tremors spread, my elbows started to shake. I recognized the voice as soon as I heard it, but I should have known at once, and I guess maybe in a strange way I did know. Jordan Phelps, out of jail already, the murdering bastard, he might look older now, but he was just the same. Hanging over the rail, hurling curses at the Lions, somehow getting half a dozen fans to join in his tirade.

When the shock had worn off and I had control of my limbs again, I thought, before this game is over — right now — I'm going to run down those stairs, time it so he's leaning over the rail, catch him by the ankles, drop him onto the field. Let the Lions kick the shit out of him. Tear him limb from limb.

The stairs were filling up by the time I got to the end of the aisle, but I could see that Jordan Phelps was still slinging curses from the rail. The Rider drive must've petered out because there were more and more people filing out, flowing down the stairs, and I let them carry me along until I stepped onto the landing at the bottom, squeezing between two men and close to the rail.

Directly behind Jordan Phelps.

Four of the Lions were standing right beneath him now, shouting back at him, and he was leaning so far over the rail all I had to do was give him a bump and he was gone. Let the Lions beat the snot out of him.

But no, a revenge fantasy, that's all it was. Satisfying in a way, but just a stupid fantasy.

Still, I had to do something.

Why not tap him casually on the shoulder, let him see I knew who he was, tell him exactly what I thought of him? Sure, tell him, "Well, Phelps, it looks to me like Anna had you pegged just right. You're still an asshole."

I had to tap him twice before he turned around.

"What the hell you want?" His eyes dark and hard, his mouth set in a frown, as if his expression had been glazed and fired in a kiln. He had no idea who I was.

"You're Jordan Phelps," I said. "Anna Big Sky had it right when she called — "

He swung at me then, a roundhouse right, but I stepped back and his fist whistled past my chin. My heart was pounding, but I stood and faced him.

Jordan Phelps took a step toward me, paused, disgruntled fans stepping around us, between us, and down the stairs. For once in his life, he looked unsure.

"No," he said, "no, you're the real asshole."

I had to smile at that — as soon as I mentioned Anna he knew what I was going to say. I could have called him something else, but what was the point of exchanging insults with someone like Jordan Phelps? I shook my head in disgust, with myself as much as with him, took a couple of deep breaths, and walked down the stairs. Left him standing there like an actor who'd forgotten all his lines.

Going near him was a mistake. What I should have done was stay in my seat, forget about stupid teen-age fantasies and play it like an adult.

Well, the game was over now, I'd follow the crowd out of Mosaic Place, meet the guys back at the car, and hope I never saw Jordan Phelps again. Hope he wasn't going to occupy my thoughts for months this time around.

Lord knows, he'd already been there far too long.

And he's there now. The football game over hours ago, I'm back in Saskatoon, in a turmoil once again, thinking about that horrible October. My father struggling to ease my suffering in any way he could, relying, naturally, on what had meant so much to him, the wisdom of the Bible, trying to pass it on to me, a boy who didn't want to listen. No matter how many hours my father spent pouring over scripture, seeking passages that might speak to me, he wasn't getting through. He knew it, and he wouldn't quit. Somehow he needed to convince me that I mustn't blame myself for what had happened to my brother.

I turn and turn in bed, stare at the ceiling, the walls, the dim light seeping from the edges of the curtain. My brother dead and Jordan Phelps alive, free to go wherever he wants, attend football games, heap curses on anyone he chooses. If there are answers to be found, they dwell far beyond me, awake or asleep.

I think of my father then, and suddenly I'm smiling. "Shit happens," he once told me, the words so unlike any I had heard him utter, before or since. It must have been a battle for him to get them out.

Someday I'll have to thank him for the effort.

No, not some day. Now. I pick up the phone and dial. "Hey, Dad, it's me."

Acknowledgements

Thanks to Dave Oswald Mitchell who, when he was in high school, wrote the poem that eventually inspired this novel. Special thanks to the members of my prose group (Byrna Barclay, Pat Krause, Dave Margoshes, and Brenda Niskala) for their chapter-by-chapter feedback over a period of many months, and especially to Dave who later gave me detailed comments on the whole works. Thanks also to Geoffrey Ursell, Barbara Sapergia and T. F. Rigelhof for their readings of the manuscript. I owe debts of gratitude to R. P. MacIntyre both for recommending my manuscript to the publisher and for his many editorial insights, and, of course, to the good folks at Thistledown for turning the manuscript into a book. Additional thanks to Karon Selzer and the staff of the Moose Jaw Public Library for their assistance and support. And finally a tip of the hat to the Saskatchewan Writers Guild, whose staff and members have helped sustain me through many years of writing.

Robert Currie is a poet and fiction writer who lives in Moose Jaw where he taught for thirty years at Central Collegiate, winning the Joseph Duffy Memorial Award for excellence in teaching language arts. He also taught creative writing for four summers at the Saskatchewan School of the Arts in Fort San and for three summers at the Sage Hill Writing Experience in Lumsden. He is the author of ten books, including the short story collections, *Night Games* and *Things You Don't Forget,* and the novel, *Teaching Mr Cutler.*